Loving
Spirit

Lind. .pman lives in Leicestershire with her family a ' two dogs. When she is not writing, she spends h time looking after her three children, readin; .king to people about writing, and horse riding v never she can.

You ca d out more about Linda on her websites at *lin .. .pman.co.uk* and *lindachapmanauthor. :o.uk*

Books by Linda Chapman

Loving Spirit

Linda Chapman

Loving Spirit

PUFFIN

PUFFIN BOOKS

Published by the Penguin Group
Penguin Books Ltd, 80 Strand, London WC2R ORL, England
Penguin Group (USA) Inc., 375 Hudson Street, New York, New York 10014, USA
Penguin Group (Canada), 90 Eglinton Avenue East, Suite 700, Toronto, Ontario, Canada M4P 2Y3
(a division of Pearson Penguin Canada Inc.)
Penguin Ireland, 25 St Stephen's Green, Dublin 2, Ireland (a division of Penguin Books Ltd)
Penguin Group (Australia), 250 Camberwell Road, Camberwell, Victoria 3124, Australia
(a division of Pearson Australia Group Pty Ltd)
Penguin Books India Pvt Ltd, 11 Community Centre, Panchsheel Park, New Delhi – 110 017, India
Penguin Group (NZ), 67 Apollo Drive, Rosedale, North Shore 0632, New Zealand
(a division of Pearson New Zealand Ltd)
Penguin Books (South Africa) (Pty) Ltd, 24 Sturdee Avenue, Rosebank, Johannesburg 2196, South Africa

Penguin Books Ltd, Registered Offices: 80 Strand, London WC2R ORL, England

puffinbooks.com

First published 2010

3

Text copyright © Linda Chapman, 2010
All rights reserved

The moral right of the author has been asserted

Set in Sabon 12/16pt
Typeset by Palimpsest Book Production Limited, Falkirk, Stirlingshire
Made and printed in England by Clays Ltd, St Ives plc

British Library Cataloguing in Publication Data
A CIP catalogue record for this book is available from the British Library

ISBN: 978-0-141-32832-4

www.greenpenguin.co.uk

Penguin Books is committed to a sustainable future
for our business, our readers and our planet.
The book in your hands is made from paper
certified by the Forest Stewardship Council.

Listen and I will speak
Ask and I will answer

Spirit . . .

The grey horse and Ellie faced each other in the stable. The horse was still, his long forelock falling over his eyes. His mane, once so tangled, reached halfway down his neck. He snorted quietly, the curved tips of his pricked ears almost meeting. Ellie felt a rush of intense love as she looked at him, love so sharp it almost hurt.

Mine, she thought. *For always.*

She and the horse belonged together. They had from the first moment they'd met. Ellie breathed in and out, calming and centring herself, letting her own unhappiness go, sending out great waves of affection.

I'm here, she told the horse in her mind. *I love you. I'll listen.*

Stretching out his muzzle, the grey horse touched her hands. A stream of vivid images flooded into Ellie's head – the horse being ridden up a stony track, one shoe missing, tack stiff with grease and sweat.

She could feel her own back aching, just as his had with the large man riding him. She winced as she felt the reins pull back and the metal bit bang into his teeth. She heard the cursing from the rider and the swish of the stick as it lashed down. The horse's confusion and pain broke over her. Why was the man hitting him? Why was he shouting?

Please stop. Please. I'm trying . . .

She was lost in the horse's memories and feelings. Outside the stable, the wind blew down from the high peaks of the mountains, bending the bare branches of the trees and blowing up the fleeces of the black-faced sheep that huddled together near the stone walls. Wet flakes of sleet started to fall from the heavy sky, but in the stable Ellie didn't notice. The rest of the world had faded away. It was just her and her horse . . .

Two months earlier . . .

Chapter One

The estate car chugged along the steep, narrow lane, its green paint hidden beneath layers of mud. Ellie Carrington sat in the front, her feet jostling for space with old drink cans, empty sandwich packets, a grooming brush with hardly any bristles left and a frayed red headcollar. She hugged her arms over her chest and stared out of the window at the hilly countryside they were driving through.

Falling-down stone walls divided the fields, topped with loose strands of barbed wire. Many of the fields were bare and empty. In others, sheep grazed the short grass, their fleeces a dirty grey-brown colour, their backs turned against the wind. In the fields lower down the mountains, a few shaggy cattle were grazing.

I hate it, thought Ellie bleakly, looking at the snow-capped peaks to her left. *I hate it here.*

An image of the lush meadows and the rolling hills of her home in New Zealand filled her mind. *Not home*. Her grey-blue eyes prickled as the thought slammed into her. *Not any more.*

She stared fixedly out of the window and began to wind a strand of her long, wavy blonde hair round her index finger, counting in her head with each turn. By the time she reached seven, the band of hair was beginning to cut off the feeling in her finger, but thankfully the tears had started to sink down inside her again and she was back to just feeling numb. Numb was good. It was better than hurting. In the last six months she'd learnt lots of little ways like that to stop herself crying.

The day her life had changed seemed both like yesterday but also a lifetime away. She'd been at the stables where she kept her pony, Abbey, and where her mum kept her three horses. She'd been there with her best friend, Rachel. Ellie's parents had gone away for the weekend together, so she'd arranged to stay with Rachel that night. But from the moment Rachel's mum had arrived at the yard, much earlier than arranged, Ellie had known that something was wrong. She knew she would never forget the words Rachel's mum had said: *Ellie, honey. There's been an accident . . .*

She had gone on to explain how a truck had skidded across the road that Ellie's mum and dad were driving along. Their car had been hit and they had both died instantly.

Ellie could barely remember the months following. They were just a blur, moving out of her house, selling the horses, the discussions over where she should live. Her dad had been English, and had an older brother, Len, who lived in England still. Her mother was an only child from New Zealand. At first, Ellie went to live a short distance away with her New Zealand grandma, but she was old and not very well. A month ago her gran had fallen and needed a serious hip operation, and it had been decided that Ellie would move to England to live with Len at the start of the next year.

'It'll be the best thing for you, sweetheart,' her grandma had said. 'You'll be with your uncle and cousin – Joe's sixteen, only a year and a half older than you, and you'll be living on a horse farm. Your uncle shows horses and ponies. Think how much you'll like that.'

Ellie had loved horses ever since she could remember, but even the thought of living with horses wasn't enough to persuade her. 'I don't care. I don't want to go to England. I want to stay here with you. I can help look after you, Gran. Don't send me away,' she'd begged.

She'd heard the unhappiness in her gran's voice. 'The doctor says I'll be in hospital for a long while and then a nursing home. You have to go, Ellie. I'm sorry.'

None of Ellie's arguments had made the slightest difference. Her grandmother and the other people in charge of her parents' will had decided it was best that she went to live in England. She was fourteen and had no power to change their minds.

So here I am, Ellie thought, staring desolately out of the window.

She thought of Abbey, her pony, who had been sold, and a lump started to form in her throat. They had found a good home for the mare with two young girls – really she had become too small for Ellie in the last year and would have had to be sold anyway, but Ellie had thought she would get another pony. Now she had nothing. Just herself and her suitcases.

She looked across at her Uncle Len. His face was lined and weather-beaten, his hair cut so short he almost looked bald. His eyes were the same grey-blue as Ellie's, but they were hard. He hadn't said much to her when he'd collected her at the airport, just looked her up and down as she came through customs with the flight attendant who had been looking after her. 'You got here all right then?' he'd said in his gruff accent.

Ellie hadn't really known what to say to that. It wasn't a proper question. Of course she'd got there, otherwise she wouldn't be standing in front of him. Desperately miserable, she'd just nodded.

'Car's this way.' He'd signed the flight attendant's forms, taken the handle of her trolley and then set off towards the car park.

The flight attendant had called goodbye. Ellie thanked her and then hurried after her uncle.

She studied him now across the car. She had never heard much about Uncle Len; she just knew that her dad, who had been four years younger, had never really got on with him. They had written once a year at Christmas, but otherwise hadn't kept in touch and never visited each other. Her dad had gone to university, become a vet and then moved to New Zealand, whereas her uncle had left school as soon as he could, gone to work at a racing yard and now had his own stables in north Derbyshire near to where they had both grown up. The only thing the two of them seemed to have in common was that they had both chosen to work with animals. Looking at her uncle's set face, Ellie felt glad that he wasn't more like her dad; it would have been much harder to be with him if she was reminded of Dad all the time. She missed both her parents so intensely – her energetic, bubbly mum who had been a kindergarten teacher, and her quieter, more thoughtful father. She had often travelled around with him as he had done his vet rounds, seeing the animals, helping out. She stopped her thoughts there as the tears threatened again.

Len seemed to sense her gaze and glanced across. Ellie dropped her eyes to her lap. But now eye contact had been made, the silence suddenly seemed to fill the car.

'How . . . how many horses do you have?' she asked, to break it.

'Twenty-nine on the yard, some liveries, some mine,' he answered. 'You ride, don't you?'

She nodded.

'Then you'll ride the smaller ponies for me,' he said. 'You're a good size for them.'

'Ponies?' Ellie echoed.

'Four-legged creatures, head at one end, tail at the other, hay goes in, muck comes out.'

Ellie's cheeks coloured. From some people the comment might have been a joke, but her uncle didn't seem the joking sort.

'You'll have to make yourself useful if you're staying with me,' he went on. 'You'll work just like everyone else. You'll ride the ponies in the shows and when we have buyers round, and then you'll work on the yard like we all do.'

Ellie disliked the tone of his voice, but she had no energy to fight right then. She just wanted to be left alone. She shrugged, wrapping her arms tighter around herself.

Her uncle turned his gaze back to the road.

*

After another twenty minutes of driving through small villages with grey stone houses, the road twisted round a corner and began to head downwards again. There was a town just visible in the valley below. Len pointed across the fields to the left where there was an old farmhouse nestling beneath a ridge of bare-branched trees on the mountainside. 'That's it,' he said. 'That's your new home.'

Ellie swallowed at the word as her eyes took in the farmhouse. It was three storeys high. There was a large courtyard of stables and two big horse barns with stalls inside. Behind the barns the land had been levelled and there was an outdoor all-weather ring and a field with bright jumps in, the only splash of colour on the green and grey landscape. She could see horses and ponies grazing on the hillsides, wearing waterproof rugs and hoods over their necks.

Len turned the car down a bumpy lane with a white and black sign saying *High Peak Stables*. As the car jolted over the rough pot-holed surface, Ellie looked at the house looming ahead and shivered. It looked very lonely.

The drive ended in a tarmacked parking area with two horseboxes, a trailer, a motorbike and a few cars. There was a smaller outdoor school at the end of it. A dark bay pony with a white star was being trotted around. His ears were pricked and his eyes soft. The boy who was riding looked too big for the pony, but he was slimly built and he rode lightly. Sitting down in the saddle, he moved the pony into a flowing canter.

Despite her unhappiness, Ellie couldn't help but catch her breath. The pony reminded her slightly of Abbey, who had been a dark bay with a white star too. 'That pony's gorgeous,' she murmured.

Her uncle nodded briefly as he parked the car. 'That's Picasso. He's only six but he took every novice 143-centimetre working hunter pony class he entered last year and went Champion at the BSPS Summer Champs. Got his Horse of the Year show ticket first time out and took third place there in October.' His eyes narrowed appreciatively. 'Not bad for a pony picked up for £500 as a four-year-old.'

Ellie didn't know what half of what her uncle had just said meant, but she didn't really care. She wasn't interested in what the pony had won; she was just captivated by its beauty and grace.

Her uncle got out and Ellie opened her door. The cold wind whipped her tangled hair away from her face. The boy cantered to the fence and slowed the pony to an easy halt. Pushing her hands into the pockets of her fleece jacket, Ellie followed her uncle over.

'He's going all right.' Her uncle gave a satisfied nod.

The boy looked relieved.

'This is your cousin, Ellie,' Len told him.

'Hi, Ellie.' The boy's hair was sandy brown, his eyes dark greeny-grey. 'I'm Joe.'

His smile was warm and Ellie felt a rush of relief. 'Hi,' she said.

'How long was your flight then?' Joe asked her.

'Twenty-four hours.'

'You must be whacked.'

'She wasn't flying the plane herself, Joe,' Len said abruptly. 'She was probably asleep most of it. Go on now, get working that pony again. Where's Luke?'

'He's in the wash-barn, clipping.' Joe smiled at Ellie. 'I'll catch you later,' he said, moving the pony on.

'Right, lass, come and see round.' Len strode back up the car park and on to the large rectangular court-yard, which had ten spacious loose boxes, arranged on two sides. The third side had a tackroom, a rug room and a wash-stall, and the fourth side was the wall of a large airy barn. Everywhere was immaculate. Ellie gazed round at the horses who were looking out over their doors. They were all beautiful – greys, bays, chestnuts.

'The main show horses have stables here,' said Len, pointing around the courtyard. 'The barn at the side there has the livery and younger horses, and the barn further up towards the ring is for the ponies.

There're three foaling boxes round the back too.' A man in his forties with a bald head pushed a wheelbarrow across the yard. 'That's Stuart, ex-jockey,' Len went on. 'He's been my yard manager now for ten years. You'll meet the other grooms later – Helen and Sasha – and you'll mind you do what they say.'

Ellie bristled slightly at his tone, but just then a tall boy who looked about eighteen came to the open door of the wash-stall. He had a pair of electric clippers in one hand and his jeans were covered with horsehair. A sandy terrier-type dog bounced around his heels, chewing at his boots.

'That's Luke,' said Len, walking towards him.

Ellie wondered who Luke was. Maybe he was another groom? His dark hair was slightly long and there was a swagger to his step. As she and Len reached him, Luke's deep-blue eyes swept over Ellie assessingly and she felt something tighten inside her. Though he hadn't even spoken yet, she felt a prickle of dislike. The dog came trotting over to her and Ellie bent down to pat it.

'Luke, this is Ellie,' Len said.

Ellie glanced up and met Luke's appraising gaze.

'I thought she was supposed to be fourteen,' he said to Len.

'Just small for her age,' Len replied. 'Useful, though. Means she can ride the fourteen-handers – and exercise the smaller ponies.'

'Yeah, guess there's that,' agreed Luke. 'Now Joe's not such a midget we need someone else. So she can ride then?'

Ellie stared at both of them. They were talking about her as if she wasn't there! 'Yes, actually, I can ride,' she put in before Len could speak. She could feel her temper rising, breaking through her numbness. 'I've ridden since I was three. I had my own pony, you know.'

'Oh.' Luke raised his eyebrows. 'So you're the expert then? I'll know who to come to if I want any advice.' His eyes mocked her.

Ellie glared at him.

'Did you see to the kittens then?' Len asked him.

'Not yet. They're in here still,' Luke said, breaking eye contact with Ellie and jerking a thumb behind him.

'Kittens!' Ellie hurried to the door. She loved cats almost as much as ponies. There were some bales of straw inside, and in a pile of loose straw in the corner was a black mother cat with three very tiny baby kittens, their heads looking comically big compared to their small black bodies. 'They're so cute,' she breathed as she watched the kittens padding round and feeding from the mother. 'Can I pick one up?' she asked Len eagerly.

'No,' he replied. 'We'll get your stuff in from the car. See to them, Luke.'

Ellie followed her uncle silently back to the car. The cases were heavy, but Len carried one in each hand easily over to the house while Ellie carried her rucksack and hand-luggage bag.

The house was very old, with white windows that held little rectangular panes of glass. Yellow lichen was growing on some of the stone. Inside, there were no flowers or plants, no pictures on the walls; the only photos or ornaments were of horses. The kitchen was large with a quarry-tiled floor, a pine table and a bay window. It was clean but bare, apart from the clutter of horse and motorbike magazines on the window seat, and a television. There was a lounge leading off it, containing a threadbare sofa with no cushions, a couple of armchairs and another, even bigger, television. The hallway was empty apart from a mirror and a wooden staircase with a ragged carpet runner. It had the feeling of a house lived in just by men. *But then that's what it is*, Ellie reminded herself. She knew that Len had got divorced eight years ago. There was only him and Joe here now.

There were three bedrooms on the first floor. But Len didn't stop. He continued up another flight of stairs.

'You'll be up here,' he told her.

Ellie shivered as they reached the second floor. There was a feeling of damp in the air. Len showed her into a cold room that had a single bed with a white cover, an old dark wardrobe and a dark chest of drawers with a round mirror on top of it, and an empty black fireplace. It was like something from a history book.

'This is my room?' Ellie said uncertainly.

Len nodded. 'Bathroom's down the corridor. I'll leave you to unpack. Come down when you're done.'

He walked back down the stairs. For a moment, Ellie just stood there, her eyes taking in the strange room, and then desolation broke through her defences. She had lost everything and now she had to live here, like this. She started to cry, covering her face with her hands, her body shaking, but trying not to make a sound. The last thing she wanted was for her Uncle Len to hear and come back. From the little she had seen of him, she was sure she would get no sympathy at all.

At last the storm of tears dried up. Taking several deep breaths, and aching with loneliness, Ellie went to the bathroom. It had a cold lino floor, a plain white bath, a sink and toilet, a plastic bath mat and a shower attached to the bath. It was completely bare, with just a single old grey towel to soften it.

At least I don't have to share it with anyone else, she thought, splashing freezing water from the cold tap over her face and trying to be positive. *Maybe I can make it look good. I could buy things. Do it up.*

She had money. Before she'd left New Zealand, her grandma had made sure she had some in case she needed to buy anything.

'Your uncle might not understand about the clothes and things girls need to buy,' she'd said to her. 'There's the money you inherited from your parents. It's in trust for you until you get older, but if you need things just write. As long as it's a reasonable request, no one's going to keep the money from you. See how you go, but take this to start. It's a lot of money so be careful with it.' And she'd pressed the money into Ellie's hands. It had looked like toy money to Ellie, nothing like the New Zealand banknotes she was used to. She'd counted it later and found her gran had given her three hundred pounds. Maybe she could use some of it to buy a few things to make her bedroom and bathroom look better.

Yeah, I'll do it, she thought, feeling a flicker of her old energy. *I'm not going to live like this.*

Feeling slightly calmer, she went to the window of her bedroom. Below her were the stables. As she watched, Luke came out of the barn, a sack in his hands.

What was in it? It looked heavy at the bottom, as if it had weights in or something, but the middle of it seemed to be moving.

Ellie opened the window and heard the yard

manager, Stuart, calling to Luke. 'You got those kittens then?'

Luke looked at the sack. 'Yeah, they're here. I'll use the pond in the upper field. It's good and deep.'

Ellie's heart lurched. *No!* She remembered her uncle's words: *See to them, Luke.* The next minute she was flying down the stairs.

Chapter Two

Ellie tore out of the house. Joe had brought Picasso in from the school and was untacking him.

'What's he doing?' Ellie gasped, pointing at Luke as he disappeared round the barn. 'Is he really going to drown those kittens?' For a moment, she hoped, prayed, that she'd got it wrong.

But as soon as she saw the look of unhappiness cross Joe's face she knew she hadn't. He nodded.

'Well, stop him!' Ellie cried, her anger overcoming her other feelings. All she thought about were the little black kittens in the sack on Luke's back.

Joe shook his head. 'I can't stop him. It's Dad's orders.'

'So?' Ellie stared at him in disbelief. 'You can't let it happen! You can't let him just kill them.'

Joe didn't move.

Giving up on him, Ellie raced after Luke. As she ran round the stable block, she saw him striding across a field. He reached the pond and pulled the sack from his back.

'No!' Ellie screamed as he chucked it into the water.

Luke looked over his shoulder in surprise. She ran towards him. 'Get them out!' she cried furiously. 'You can't do that!'

Luke just shrugged.

Seeing it was no use trying to persuade him, she flung off her fleece and, heedless of the cold water, began wading into the pond.

'Are you crazy? What are you doing?' Luke yelled, his air of cool momentarily leaving him.

'I'm going to rescue them!' Ellie shot back, her eyes scanning the water as she tried to see where they'd gone. Panic welled up inside her. They'd be drowning! 'Help me!'

'There's no point. They'll be dead by the time you get them.' Luke turned round and started to walk away.

Ellie yelled a swear word at him and waded out further. The icy water was up to her thighs now. She reached down desperately. Where were the kittens? Her foot struck something soft. She bent down. It was the sack! Gasping, she used all her strength to yank it out of the water and drag it back to the bank. Her clothes were soaked through, but she didn't care. She'd got the kittens! *If they're still alive*, she thought, her stomach turning over.

Pushing through the water as quickly as she could, she reached the bank. She struggled to find her footing, but then someone grasped her wrist. She jumped, her eyes flying upwards. Had Luke come back? She met Joe's dark-green gaze instead.

'Here.' He half pulled her out of the water, taking the sack from her. She glared at him. She hadn't forgotten how he'd refused to help back on the yard. Taking the sack, he placed it gently down.

'You shouldn't have done that,' he said anxiously. 'Dad'll be mad.'

'I don't care!' Ellie declared, through teeth that were starting to chatter. She threw herself down on to her knees and started to pull frantically at the string that was tying the neck of the sack.

'Wait.' Joe took a penknife out of his pocket and cut swiftly through it. In an instant, the sack fell open. Feeling sick, not knowing what she would see, Ellie peered inside. Two of the kittens were lying lifeless on the bricks that weighted the bottom of the sack. She saw instantly that she couldn't help them now, but the third was moving weakly, coughing up pond water. She pulled it out and held it to her chest. She had often seen her dad with baby lambs when they had been born half dead, barely breathing.

'Give me my fleece!' she snapped, too upset to be polite.

Joe handed it across without a word. Ellie wrapped

the kitten in it and, shielding it with her body from the cold wind, began to rub at its skin with the inside of the fleece. It coughed and spluttered. Working in small circles, she rubbed it all over, drying it, warming it. As she did so, Joe hurried away.

'Fine. You go too. You're just as bad as them!' she muttered.

Bending her head, she continued working on the kitten. She was shivering herself, but she ignored the cold that felt like it was sinking through to her bones. 'I hate them,' she whispered to it, a sob catching in her throat. 'I hate them all! How could they do that to you?'

She rubbed until the kitten's body felt warm and then she wrapped her hands round it and, shutting her eyes, held it tight. She had always tried to help ill and weak animals. *You'll get better*, she willed it.

Ellie tried to clear the anger from her mind, and concentrated on letting love flow from her to the kitten, imagining it warming the kitten, helping it . . .

Suddenly she felt something being put round her shoulders. She looked up and saw Joe behind her. One hand was draping the thick golden stable rug round her; in his other arm he was holding the black mother cat. She mewed loudly and struggled when she saw her baby.

'Is it still alive?' he asked.

As he spoke, the kitten's rough tongue rasped over Ellie's fingers.

'Yes,' she replied briefly.

'Then the best place for it is with its mum,' he said. 'Look, let's take it to the hay barn over there.' He motioned to a stone building at the back of the stables. 'That's where the extra hay and straw is kept. We can put them in there on top of the bales. No one will go up there for at least the next month now. By the time they do, the kitten will be able to fend for itself and people will probably just think it's one of the other cats on the yard.'

Ellie gave him a wary look. She had been so busy hating him along with Len and Luke; it was hard now to trust him.

His eyes met hers. 'I'm sorry I didn't help before. Come on,' he said, reaching out his hand.

Ellie hesitated and then let him help her up.

Half an hour later, they sat together under the low roof of the loft of the hay barn, watching the cats. Ellie had the rug wrapped round her, warmer now despite her wet clothes. The mother cat, who Joe had said was called Poppy, and the black kitten who Ellie had now named Sweep, were lying together in a nest of warm hay. The kitten had fed and both cats were asleep.

'I wish I could have saved them all,' said Ellie softly.

'You'd better hope that Dad doesn't find out you saved this one,' said Joe, running a hand through his hair. 'It'll be best to tell him they all drowned, or he'll get hold of Sweep and drown him himself.'

'But why?' Ellie looked at him in bewilderment. 'Why be so cruel?'

'It was an inbred litter. The kittens were weak, not healthy. You can see Sweep's head.'

Ellie looked at the little kitten. His head was set at a slightly wonky angle. 'It's no reason to kill him.'

'It is to Dad. Animals are a business to him and he won't put up with weaklings. Any animal that isn't strong and healthy and can't pay its way has to go. You'll get used to it.'

'I won't!' Ellie declared. She gave him a look full of accusation. 'You could have stopped Luke killing them. You could have moved them before, hidden them somehow. You could have saved them after he threw them in the pond, and brought them all here.'

'And what would Dad have done to me then?' said Joe.

'What do you mean?' Ellie frowned.

Joe didn't reply.

Understanding slowly dawned. 'Do you mean he'd have *hit* you?'

Joe shrugged. 'He won't stand for being disobeyed. But don't worry, he wouldn't lay a finger on a girl, though he'll shout all right if he finds out.'

Ellie felt her feelings shift. She couldn't imagine what it must be like to grow up with a father like that. Her crossness faded as she realized what Joe had to live with.

'He already thinks I'm a rubbish son,' Joe went on. 'If I couldn't ride like I do, he'd probably want to drown me too.' He sounded like he was only half joking. 'I'm a total disappointment to him – skinny, no good at sport; I was small for ages too, nothing like him. Riding's the only thing I can do well.'

'He . . . he can't really think you're useless,' said Ellie, not knowing quite what else to say.

'Oh, he does. He's told me lots of times that he wishes I was more like Luke.'

Ellie frowned. 'Who *is* Luke? Is he a groom?'

'No, he's my cousin from down south,' Joe explained. 'On the other side of my family, not your side. He's my mum's nephew. He's never got on with his own parents that well. His dad's rich and they travel around a lot. They sent him to boarding school when he was eight and he used to come here in the holidays and help out. He rang Dad about eighteen months ago and asked for a job. His parents weren't too keen on him leaving school, but, well, when Luke's set his mind to something nothing stops him . . . In the end they gave in, and he came to live and work here.'

'So he lives in the house?' Ellie's heart sank into

her toes at the thought of seeing Luke every day for breakfast, lunch and supper.

'Yep.' Joe got to his feet. 'Come on. We'd better go now. It's almost feedtime, and if I'm not there to help with the stables Dad'll wonder where I am.'

Ellie went to her room and got changed. She watched from her window as Stuart, Luke, Joe and two girl grooms settled the horses for the night. The stables were tidied up, haynets put into each one, rugs were adjusted, water buckets filled up with clean water and, at five o'clock sharp, the feeds emptied into the mangers. Half an hour later, Stuart and the girls left and Len and the boys came inside. After a little while, Ellie heard the sound of laughing from the kitchen and smelt frying bacon, and she ventured downstairs.

Her uncle was cooking. Luke was sitting at the table, talking to him and drinking a bottle of beer. The dog was on Luke's knee, lying on her back and having her tummy tickled. Joe was sitting on his own in another chair, reading a copy of *Horse and Hound*.

'Here she is then. Florence bleedin' Nightingale,' Len said as Ellie walked in.

Luke laughed, which made the terrier jump up and lick his chin. 'Get down, Pip!' he said.

Joe glanced up at Ellie and motioned with his eyes for her to sit in the chair beside him. She joined him gratefully.

'Luke told me you tried to stop him from drowning those kittens,' Len said.

'It was cruel,' Ellie said, meeting her uncle's cold eyes. 'It wasn't fair.'

'Life's not fair.' Len was curt. 'They all drowned anyway, Joe said.'

Ellie nodded, thankful for Joe's lie. There was no way she was going to tell her uncle about Sweep after what Joe had told her earlier.

'Good.' Len pointed the spatula at her. 'I'll not have you interfering with my orders again. I won't hold with it. This is my yard and my house and I make the decisions. While you're under my roof, you'll do as I say. Tomorrow you'll start riding the ponies.'

Listening to the arrogance in his voice, something seemed to click inside Ellie. She lifted her chin. 'No, I won't.'

'What?' Len looked as though he felt he hadn't heard right.

Ellie realized both Joe and Luke were staring at her. She knew she was going to get into massive trouble, but so what? With grief swirling around inside her, she just didn't care. There was nothing her uncle could do to her that would make her feel worse than she did already, and much as she loved riding she hated being bossed around even more. 'I'll help out on the yard like everyone else, but I'm not going to ride the ponies for you.'

Len's body stiffened dangerously. 'You'll do as I say, missy.' His voice was low and angry.

Ellie looked stubbornly at him. 'I won't. You can't make me.'

She jumped as Len thundered. 'Get to your room!' He stepped towards her.

Ellie ran to the doorway and up the stairs. By the time she had raced up the second flight, she was beginning to run out of breath and her heart was beating fast. She shut her door and leant against it, listening in case anyone was going to follow her. But no one did. Going to the window, she sat down on the stone window ledge. The panes of glass were freezing cold. The sky was pitch black apart from the twinkling of stars. It looked a very lonely, wide, dark night. On the other side of the world, back home, it would be mid-morning in summer time. A lump formed in her throat.

Feel nothing, she reminded herself, holding on to the lessons she had learnt over the last six months. *Just feel nothing.*

Pulling her numbness like a shield around her, she got under the covers with all her clothes still on and lay there shivering until she fell asleep.

Chapter Three

When Ellie woke up, it was the middle of the night. Since her parents had died, waking up was always the worst moment for her. As she moved from sleep to wakefulness, there were always a few seconds when she felt as though everything that had happened was just a dream – a nightmare – but then reality would come rushing back and she would realize that it wasn't. Waking now in the darkness, she felt the familiar tidal wave of misery engulf her. It had all really happened. Her parents *were* dead. She was here in her new life with her uncle at High Peak Stables.

Well, he can say what he likes, but I'm not going to ride for him, she thought mutinously. *I'm not going to be bossed about.*

The determination gave her something to concentrate on, taking the edge off her misery. She was hot in all her clothes now and her long hair was sticking to her face. Getting out of bed, she turned on her bedside light. The house was very quiet. Checking her watch, she saw that it was past midnight. Ellie's stomach rumbled as she pulled some pyjamas from the drawer. She hadn't eaten since she was on the plane. With a sigh, she pulled a brush through her hair and then opened the door to go to the bathroom. She stopped. Someone had left a packet of crisps and a Kit Kat outside her door.

Joe, she realized. It had to be. Her uncle wouldn't have left them and she could hardly imagine Luke doing such a thing. She picked them up, feeling slightly warmer inside. *Thank you*, she told Joe silently, imagining him in one of the bedrooms downstairs.

Ten minutes later, she was back in bed. The empty crisp packet and biscuit wrapper lay on her bedside table. Pulling her knees up to her chest, she stared out of the window, thinking about her new life. She wasn't usually the sort of person who moaned. She was good at getting on with things. But how could she get on with living here? She didn't know the answer to that.

It was seven o'clock when Ellie woke again and she could hear the horses kicking their stable doors and whickering. She got out of bed, her feet freezing on the cold floor, and looked down at the stables.

Len, Luke and Joe were just leaving the house, and

Stuart and the other grooms were arriving. Ellie hesitated and then opened one of the drawers and pulled out her jodhpurs and a fleece. She had never been lazy in her life, and although she had no intention of riding the ponies as her uncle had ordered she also had no intention of being the only person in the house who didn't help.

When she walked out on the yard, she wondered what reaction she would get. Luke was the first to see her. 'Got over your tantrum, have you?'

She gave him what she hoped was a withering look, but Luke just laughed and turned away.

Her uncle was standing by the water trough. Steeling herself, Ellie walked over.

'So you've come out.' His voice was curt.

'What would you like me to do?' she spoke steadily, although her heart was beating fast.

'Fill the water buckets.' Len motioned with his thumb to the stables to the right. 'Start that side and work your way round.' She started off. He called after her. 'And make sure you scrub out every one.'

Len was a hard taskmaster and Ellie soon saw why everyone did as he said. He had a fierce temper and he could rip people to shreds with his tongue when his anger was roused – a horse with hooves not properly picked out, a stable not bedded down to his exacting standards, straw blowing loose on the yard.

If something wasn't right he soon let everyone know about it. In that first morning, Ellie quickly learnt to be careful. After the horses had been fed, the stalls mucked out and the yard swept, Len and Luke took two of the horses out into the ring to school them while the grooms had their breakfast, and Joe showed Ellie around, introducing her to the few livery clients who were about and showing her all the horses who were still in the stables.

'These are some of the stars of the yard,' he said, pointing out the horses in the stables round the court-yard. 'Although they're not looking their best at the moment. The ponies go to shows all through the winter but most of the horses have a break until their classes start again in March. You'll have to imagine them with a lot more muscle and a shine to their coats.' Joe gestured towards a massive grey with a noble head. 'This is Hereward, he's a heavyweight hunter. He's got a real name for himself on the county circuit. And this one . . .' He went to the smaller bright bay in the next box. 'This is Gabriel. He's an Intermediate working hunter and one of our rising stars. He got his ticket to the Horse of the Year first time out –'

'Whoa – stop!' interrupted Ellie, putting up her hands at the flood of information. 'I don't know what you're talking about. What's the difference between a hunter and a working hunter? And what's a ticket?'

Joe grinned. 'Oh, wow. You *have* got a lot to learn! OK. Hunter classes are show classes. The horses are ridden round the ring and they are judged on how suited they are to being hunters; the judges give them marks for how they move, what they look like and what they are like when they are ridden. Working hunters are kind of the same but they have to do a course of jumps as well, not show jumps but rustic ones – and they get marks for that. There are other types of classes too for hacks and riding horses; they look different from hunters.'

He moved along to the stable next to Gabriel where there was a beautiful dapple-grey mare with a fine, elegant head. 'Starlight here is a hack. Dad rides her.' He rubbed the mare's neck and she nuzzled him. 'She's done really well. She won Supreme Champion at the Horse of the Year show last October for the second year running. The aim of everyone showing is to qualify for the Horse of the Year show. When you qualify, people say that you've got your ticket. There are other important shows too. For the ponies there are the BSPS –' Joe caught Ellie's frown and grinned. 'Sorry! I mean, the British Show Pony Society winter and summer championships, as well as some other big shows. The ponies we have here are all show hunter ponies or working hunter ponies. Luke and I ride them.' He shot her a sideways look. 'Though Dad was hoping you would ride the smaller ones now.'

'He can hope,' muttered Ellie.

Joe looked at her curiously. 'Don't you like riding? Is that it? Luke reckons you must be scared.'

Ellie felt a flash of annoyance. 'I'm not scared. I love riding. I just don't like being bossed around.'

'You'll have to get used to that staying here,' Joe commented drily.

They walked round the rest of the boxes with Joe reeling off the names of the horses, and then they went to the livery barn. 'The liveries are all show animals,' Joe explained. 'Dad produces them – he teaches the riders, gets the horses into condition and takes them to shows. If the owners can't ride them, we do. We also have some horses like Gabriel whose owners *never* ride them; they just like owning horses and watching them at shows. They pay for Dad to produce them.'

Finally, they went to the pony horse barn. Ellie saw the beautiful dark bay pony that Joe had been riding the day before. 'He's so lovely,' she said, going over to him. The pony moved away and stood at the back of the stall, his expression aloof.

'He's a looker all right but not that friendly,' said Joe. 'Not like Barney here.' He went up to the liver-chestnut pony in the opposite stall who was pawing at the ground. As soon as Joe reached him, the pony butted him with his head.

Joe pointed out the clips on the stable lock. 'He's

a right Houdini – escapes at a moment's notice. He's even learnt to let the other horses out. He pulls back their bolts with his teeth and kicks their doors until the kick bolt at the bottom flips over. It's really important you put the extra locks on his door if you come out.' Joe rubbed the gelding's ears. 'You're a nightmare, aren't you, Barney?' he said with a grin. 'He's brilliant to ride, though, and won at the Horse of the Year. Dad thinks he and Picasso are both going to have a stellar year.'

'So what about the other ponies?' asked Ellie, wandering down the aisle.

'That's Milly.' Joe pointed to a small bright chestnut with a flaxen mane who looked about 13.2 hands high. 'She's a show hunter pony. And that's Gem next to her, another show hunter pony. He's only four, but Dad wants to get him out to a few shows this year so he can get used to the atmosphere. And this is Merlin.' Joe's eyes took on a new warmth as he walked over to the old bay pony. He was only about 12.2 hands high, too small to even look properly over his stall door.

Ellie leant over and patted him. 'Who does he belong to?'

'Well, he's pretty much mine. He's been here longer than any other horse or pony. He's twenty now and I learnt to ride on him. Luckily, he's good if we have kids come for showing lessons who can't bring their own ponies for some reason, and he's a good companion to the other horses. He's so calm he can be turned out with anyone. That's why Dad lets him stay. I'm glad. I never want him to go.' Joe rubbed Merlin's neck. 'You and me go back a long way, don't we, lad?'

Ellie saw the affection in Joe's eyes and smiled. She could see that he felt the same way about horses and ponies as she did.

The two of them finally headed out of the barn. The grooms were just coming out of the tackroom, having finished their breakfast. As well as Stuart, there was red-headed Helen, who was Stuart's girl-friend, and Sasha, who looked about eighteen, with straightened blonde hair and wide-set eyes in a pretty face. Ellie was observant and saw that Sasha was flirting with Luke all the time. *Not that Luke seems to mind*, Ellie noted.

'It's riding time now,' Joe explained to Ellie. 'We prepare the horses that are to be ridden today. Any horses who are being rested need to be turned out. Stuart and Dad work out which horses will be doing what and write it up on the noticeboard outside the tackroom. The afternoons are usually taken up with working the youngsters, grooming, trimming, clip-ping, and with Dad teaching people.'

'What shall I do?' Ellie asked.

'Help get the horses ready. We don't groom properly

until the afternoon, we just give them a quick tidy-up before they're ridden. Stuart will show you what to do. I'd better get Barney out and start riding or Dad'll go mad.'

At Hereward's stable, Stuart showed Ellie how Len liked the horses to be got ready for exercise in the mornings. 'If you could sort out Picasso that would be a help,' he said to her once they had finished Hereward. 'Just watch yourself when you're oiling his back hooves. He got bitten by a snake when he was younger and he's likely to jump a bit if he sees the straw moving behind him.'

Ellie went to the pony barn and set to work on Picasso. She soon found herself enjoying it as she brushed him over quickly, untangled his tail, put a tail bandage on and picked his feet out as Stuart had shown her. She finished by carefully putting hoof oil on his hooves and then rugged him up again. He stood quietly, not trying to nuzzle her or seek contact, and when she patted him she had the feeling he was tolerating it rather than enjoying it.

'I'm guessing you don't really like people, do you, boy?' she murmured. The pony regarded her, neither aggressive nor friendly. Just slightly guarded. For a moment, Ellie got the impression of an invisible prickly cloud of energy surrounding his body, keeping people away.

She often got strange feelings like that about

animals. She had done ever since she could remember. Sometimes she felt she could even tell when they were ill and what the matter was with them. She'd told her dad about it when she was little, but he'd just smiled and said it was her imagination. Ever since then, she'd tried to ignore the sensation, but sometimes, when she was alone like this with an animal, she got feelings that were so strong they were very hard to dismiss.

Shaking her head at herself, she picked up the grooming kit and went to Milly's stall. In contrast to Picasso, Milly was a feisty ball of energy who didn't want to keep still for a second; she scraped her hoof on the floor and fidgeted around, grabbing at Ellie's coat with her teeth. But Ellie didn't mind; it made her feel that tiny bit more at peace to be around ponies again, breathing in their sweet smell and making them look good. After a while, she heard Joe calling her.

He was standing outside with Barney. 'I'm going to ride Picasso now. Would you mind untacking Barney for me?'

'Sure.' Ellie took the chestnut pony back to his stall. His saddle patch was damp with sweat but the rest of him was fine. She rubbed him down and rugged him up. He chewed thoughtfully at the wood on his stable door. 'Stop it!' she scolded.

He gave her a mischievous look from under his

long forelock and proceeded to use his teeth to pull at the large plastic manger where his feed went out of its holder. He dropped it on the floor with a clatter.

'Barney!' Ellie took it from him and placed it back. Then she returned his tack to the tackroom and went to see what else she could help with.

Stuart, Helen and Sasha had got ready the horses that were going to be schooled and had taken three of the younger horses out for a hack. Ellie ended up sweeping round the muck heap. From there, she could see the rings, Joe riding Picasso and Luke riding Gabriel. Len had put three jumps out and was watching Joe and Luke ride over them. Ellie could hear his broad voice as he turned his attention on Luke whose horse was rushing slightly at the fences.

'Get him up to the bit. Circle him. Circle! Get him going forward! You're riding like a ruddy girl. Bring him round again.'

Luke didn't look bothered at all by Len's criticisms. He circled Gabriel, riding him through a series of transitions – walk to canter, canter to walk, trot to halt – asking for a new pace every few strides.

Ellie paused to watch. It was hard to tell who was the better rider, Luke or Joe. Joe was softer and lighter on the horses, asking, not telling, them what to do, and Picasso was going beautifully for him again, just as he had done the day before. But Ellie could see that Luke was also really good. He appeared to have perfect balance, controlling the horse with his long legs and strong seat. He rode effortlessly and without a hint of fear. When Gabriel was steady and listening again, Luke cantered him towards the fences and he cleared them perfectly.

'Now, that's better!' Len said approvingly.

Luke nodded. 'Put them up. He feels like he could jump six foot today.'

'He's not a flamin' show jumper,' Len responded.

'He'd jump it, though,' Luke said with a grin. 'So would I.'

'Aye, well, we all know you're a bloody lunatic.' Len grunted, but as he turned away Ellie saw a certain look of satisfaction on his face. She could see he liked Luke's style. His expression changed, though, as he turned to concentrate on Joe.

'Figure of eight at trot and canter, simple change,' he snapped as Joe trotted into the middle. 'And keep the contact with those reins!'

Joe concentrated hard, his face serious. When Len was coaching him, there was none of Len and Luke's jokey backchat.

By the time Ellie had finished sweeping, the horses were both working to Len's satisfaction. 'That'll do for Gabriel,' he said to Luke. 'Take him in. Joe, you stay for another five minutes.'

Luke rode out of the school and Pip, who had been waiting by the barn, came trotting over, stumpy blonde tail wagging. Luke's eyes passed over Ellie as if she was of no more interest than a bug. But then his hand went to his breeches' pocket. He fished his mobile out. It was buzzing. Swinging his right leg over Gabriel's neck, he jumped down and threw the reins to her. 'Here. I've got a call. Take him.'

'And what did your last slave die of?' she muttered, grabbing Gabriel. Luke wasn't listening. He'd already taken his hat off and flicked the phone open.

'Yeah? Oh, hi, babe,' he said, his voice suddenly warm. 'How are you doing?' There was a silence and then he gave a short laugh. 'Yeah. Me too.'

Luke sauntered up and down, running a hand through his dark hair. Ellie shot him a glare. Suddenly the phone buzzed again. Luke checked the display as he was talking.

'Sorry, look, Issy. I've got to run. Catch you later. Yeah, I will. Missing you already.' He clicked the END CALL button and then clicked CALL ANSWER. 'Hi, Jodie,' he said. 'Long time no see. So where have you been hiding yourself?'

Ellie rolled her eyes. Honestly! Gabriel rubbed his face against her and she patted his neck. 'Come on, I'll take you to your stable.'

Just then, Stuart, Helen and Sasha came back. But

as they reached the yard there was a clatter of hooves and two chestnut ponies came trotting out of the pony barn.

'Barney's out!' shouted Stuart in alarm.

'So's Milly!' cried Helen, already jumping off the horse she was riding and chucking the reins to Sasha.

Ellie's hand flew to her mouth, as she instantly realized what had happened. She'd forgotten Joe's warning about putting the extra lock on Barney's door. 'Here!' she gasped, pushing Gabriel's reins into Luke's hands.

'What are you doing?' Luke demanded.

'Barney and Milly have got out!'

She raced to help. The two ponies were dodging out of the way of Stuart and Helen. Barney trotted round, tail and head held high. Milly cantered to a patch of grass and began to grab at it.

'Here, boy,' said Helen, approaching Barney with her hand outstretched. But he just shook his head and trotted away, while Milly let Stuart get within a few metres and then shied and trotted after Barney. Ellie tried to head her off, but she plunged away, stopping only to investigate an empty bucket on its side. As she did so, she stepped through the metal handle. Giving a snort, she jumped back with it caught round her hoof. She ran backwards in alarm, stopping only when she reached the fence and then stamping until it came off. Ellie stood helplessly, not knowing what to do. From behind her she could hear Len swearing loudly. He had heard the noise and come out of the ring with Joe to see what the commotion was about.

'What the flamin' heck's going on? Who let that ruddy pony out?' he bellowed. 'And why are you all standing round like gormless halfwits? Someone get hold of them NOW!'

Stuart had disappeared into the barn and was coming out with a feedbucket and two leadropes. He rattled the pony nuts. 'Here, Barney lad. Come on. Here you go.' Barney stopped trotting round and pricked his ears. With a greedy whinny, he cantered over and thrust his head into the bucket. Stuart quickly threw the rope round his neck and Helen ran over to grab hold of him, while Stuart went to tempt Milly.

'Got you,' he said as Milly put her head in the bucket too.

'I'll take her,' Ellie offered.

'Oh, no,' Len said, pointing his finger at her. 'You're going nowhere, miss. I want to know exactly how that pony got out of his stable.'

Ellie met her uncle's furious gaze. 'Um . . . I . . . well . . .'

'It wasn't Ellie's fault,' Joe jumped in. 'Don't blame her, Dad. I didn't warn her about Barney and the locks.'

Ellie looked at him swiftly.

Len's eyes narrowed. 'How could you be so daft? You should have told her. You know no one works in that barn without knowing about the locks. Imagine if the ponies had got out on the road. As it is, the mare's probably lamed herself. Haven't you got a brain cell in that useless head of yours? Thick as two bloody planks you are. Flamin' –'

Ellie was unable to bear Joe being shouted at because of her for a second longer. 'It wasn't Joe's fault!' she burst out. 'He did tell me. I forgot.'

She saw Joe give a quick desperate shake of his head. The next second she realized why. Len's anger instantly turned to fury. 'You lied to me?' he said, staring at Joe. 'Of all the . . .' Stepping forward, he grabbed Joe's shirt and brought his face right up into Joe's, his eyes blazing. 'Don't you ever, *ever* lie to me!' he thundered. He shoved Joe away from him with such violence that his son fell down on the stony ground with a smack.

Ellie held in the whimper that would have escaped from her if she hadn't been terrified it would make everything worse.

Joe gingerly pulled himself up to a sitting position, but wouldn't meet anyone's eye.

Turning away, Len marched over to where Stuart was examining Milly's leg. 'What's the damage?' he said curtly.

'A small cut. Bit of swelling starting. I'll hose her down, boss.'

Len nodded and then walked towards the house, shaking his head in disgust.

For a moment there was silence. Helen led Barney into the stable block, one hand on his nose, the other holding the leadrope tight. Sasha took the others down to the yard, looking subdued.

'Well, that helped,' Luke said drily to Ellie as she ran over to try and help Joe up. But Joe shook his head at her quickly and stood up himself.

Ellie swallowed, still reeling from seeing Len lash out at Joe like that. It was all her fault.

'Leave it out, Luke,' Joe muttered, his face red.

Luke shrugged his shoulders and walked away.

Ellie looked at Joe. 'Joe . . . I'm . . . I'm sorry.'

He took a breath. 'Don't worry. I've had worse.'

'I just wanted to stop him.'

'Look, forget it,' Joe said. 'Just don't leave the lock off Barney's door again, OK?'

'Never,' Ellie promised, still feeling awful.

Joe managed a smile. 'Don't look like that. It's fine. I'd better go and untack Picasso before he puts a foot through his reins. God knows what would happen then. Why don't you go and see if Stuart needs a hand with Milly?'

He walked away, leaving Ellie standing on the slope, overwhelmed by a mixture of emotions –

misery, guilt, hatred of her uncle and the urge to run, it didn't matter where, she just wanted to get far, far away. Across the wintery fields, she could see the bare peaks. The desolate grey sky pressed down with just a single bird flying across it. She wished with all her heart that she could be somewhere – anywhere – else.

Chapter Four

Over the next month Ellie gradually got used to living at High Peak Stables. She tried not to think about her parents and the numbness settled back over her, sealing around her in a protective layer. She worked hard, hiding her unhappiness as best she could, avoiding Len and Luke. Len had his hands full with the horses and the clients he taught, and Luke was far too busy to take much notice of her, flirting with Sasha and the female livery owners who kept their horses at the yard, taking phone calls and working with the horses. He strode around the yard in the day, exuding a relentless energy, with Pip scampering at his heels, before going off on his motorbike into town in the evenings. It didn't seem to matter how late Luke stayed out, he was still up and on the yard by seven the next morning before doing a full day's work. But despite all the girls who seemed to fall for his charms, the only person or animal Ellie ever saw him show real affection for was Pip.

It was a busy yard, particularly in the afternoons when the livery owners came to ride their horses. There was Eliza Peterson and her friend Carey Moss who were in their twenties, a lady called Veronica Armstrong whose ten-year-old son and four-year-old daughter rode ponies Len produced, and then there were the owners who never rode but just liked to own show horses. Ellie generally kept out of the clients' way, preferring to spend time with the horses and Joe. And she had started school – a modern comprehensive in the nearby town where Joe was in the year above her. Everyone in her year had friends already, but that was OK. She just kept her head down and avoided trouble, wanting to get to the end of the school day as quickly as possible so she could get back on the yard.

The horses and Joe were the only good things in her new life at High Peak Stables. No matter how bleak she felt, the horses always helped. Their presence comforted her, and seeing to their needs took her out of her own head for a little while. A part of her wished she hadn't decided to make the stand she had. It was hard being around them and never riding. But there was no way she was going to back down and it was enough that she was around horses. Joe helped her too. Sensitive, friendly and responsible, he was the complete opposite of Luke, and the more she got to know him, the more she liked him. When there were quiet moments, they would retreat to the barn, play with Sweep the kitten, talk about the horses and music, and tease each other. During those times, Ellie felt almost normal again.

'If you had to be a dog or a cat, which would you be?' Ellie said one Saturday lunchtime as they sat together in the barn on top of the hay bales.

As Joe considered the question, she thought how lucky she was that he just seemed to get her and she almost never had to explain what she meant.

'I'd be a dog,' Joe decided. 'A Labrador.' He grinned. 'And you, you'd be one of those little white poodles with hair all tied up.'

Ellie shoved him. 'I so wouldn't!' She knew Joe was teasing her. 'Go on, what would I be?' she challenged him.

'You'd be a . . .' Joe looked at her thoughtfully. 'A dog like Pip. Interested in everything, full of energy and loyal.'

'Totally wrong, actually. I wouldn't be any type of dog, I'd be a cat,' said Ellie, running a piece of straw along the bale for Sweep to chase. The kitten pounced and she scooped him up, lying back with him. 'I'd be just like you, Sweep.'

'Yeah, with a wonky head!' Joe grinned.

Ellie frowned. 'Sweep's head isn't that wonky now.' She kissed the kitten's nose. 'You take no notice of him, Sweep. You're beautiful.' She put Sweep down and watched him bound away. 'I like it up here,' she said, glancing up at the roof of the barn. The beams were hung with years of cobwebs and dust, but it had a warm, safe feel.

'You'd better make the most of it. In another month or two there'll be shows every weekend, some in the week too. We won't get a second to sit around like this.'

There was a note in Joe's voice that suggested he wasn't looking forward to it. 'Don't you like shows?' Ellie asked curiously.

Joe shrugged. 'They're OK, I suppose, but I'd far rather be working with the horses on the yard.'

'What will you do when you leave school?' Ellie had heard Joe talking of leaving school after his GCSE exams in the summer.

'Work here I guess, though –' Joe broke off.

'What?'

'What I'd really like to do is go and work on a different yard. Not a showing one. One where they treat difficult horses, maybe, and help them.'

'That would be brilliant,' enthused Ellie. She could just see Joe doing it. 'You must.'

'Can you really imagine Dad letting me?'

Ellie frowned. 'If you want to do it, you shouldn't let him stop you.'

'Easy to say.' Joe shot her a sideways look. 'Though, actually, if it were you, you probably would just go ahead and do it anyway.' He smiled suddenly. 'I think it's cool what you're doing, Ellie. Dad's mad that you still aren't riding the ponies but what can he do? And you work hard so he can't complain.'

Ellie didn't say anything. She was beginning to find it harder and harder to be on the yard so much and yet not ride. But there was no way she would give in. A bit of her knew that it was goading her uncle and she felt a secret, silent pleasure in that. She didn't think she'd ever met anyone she liked less than her Uncle Len. He might be good with the horses, but everything she'd seen in the first day had been confirmed – with people he was badgering and domineering, expecting them to do exactly what he said.

She sighed. 'I'm so glad *you're* here,' she said to Joe. 'It would be an awful place without you.'

Joe looked pleased. 'I'm glad you're here too. It's much better than when it was just me, Dad and Luke.'

Ellie rolled her eyes. 'Luke is *so* annoying!'

Joe chuckled. 'He's not that bad. He didn't have an easy time when he was younger. His parents aren't great and he hated boarding school. And having him here keeps Dad off my back a bit.'

Ellie studied him. She knew Joe's own life hadn't been easy either. He had told her that he had really missed his mum when she left. He still saw her sometimes, just not often because she lived a long distance away in Devon and he was usually kept too busy on the yard to go and visit her.

'You know, you have to be the only girl under the sun to think Luke's annoying,' Joe went on with a certain satisfaction. 'Normally, girls all fancy him like mad.'

Ellie pulled a face. 'Ugh. No way. He's so arrogant.'

'Did you have a boyfriend in New Zealand?' Joe asked her curiously.

'Not when I left.' Ellie had been out with a few boys, but the longest she'd been out with anyone was six weeks, and since her parents had died, going out with someone had been the last thing on her mind. Her face shadowed over instantly at the thought and she had to fight back the bleakness that swelled up inside her. She stared at the bale of hay, counting to ten in her head, concentrating on the numbers as she pushed the grief back down. It was always like that. She would feel OK for a little while, not thinking about what had happened, but then something would bring it all flooding back. When she reached ten, she cleared her throat, back in control enough to speak. 'We'd better get going. Your dad will be out on the yard soon.'

Joe looked troubled. Ellie had a feeling he was about to ask her how she was and she didn't want that. She didn't want to talk about it. She climbed quickly down from the bales. 'Come on!'

But Joe wasn't to be put off. 'Are you happy here?' he said as he jumped down on to the thick layer of hay and straw that covered the barn floor.

Ellie turned back and stared at him. *Happy.* The word felt strange in her mind, as if it was a foreign language she didn't quite understand. What could she say? There were times when she felt all right, usually when she was with Joe or busy with the horses, but she never felt really and truly happy. Every night she still cried as she thought about everything she had lost. But she wasn't going to tell anyone else that, not even Joe.

'Well?' Joe pushed when she didn't reply.

'Um . . .' She saw his concerned look. 'Y-yeah. Kind of,' she stammered. 'Come on!'

She hurried off, leaving Joe watching after her, a frown on his face.

On Thursday morning Ellie was just getting ready for school when there was a knock on her bedroom door. She looked round in surprise. No one ever came up to her room. 'Who is it?'

'Me. Joe.'

Ellie opened the door. Joe grinned at her. 'I think we should have some fun today.'

She wondered what he had in mind. 'Doing what?'

'Let's bunk off school.'

'Bunk off?' Ellie echoed uncertainly. She still

54

struggled with a few of the unfamiliar English phrases. 'You mean not go to school?'

Joe nodded. 'Dad's out for the day looking at some horses. We can miss the bus and take fake notes in to say we were sick when we go back to school after half term, a week on Monday.'

Ellie stared at him, astonished. Joe was normally so conscientious and responsible, not the type of person ever to get into trouble or break rules. 'What will we do?'

'There's a horse sale on in Barrowton. We could go over there, just look at the horses, hang out for a while. I know Stuart'll take us if we ask. He's got to go into the tack shop there anyway. He won't mind going to the pub for lunch while we look round.'

'Won't he tell your dad about us missing school?'

'Not Stuart. He's not bothered by things like that. Come on,' Joe urged her. 'You need to have some fun. It'll do you good.'

A feeling of recklessness caught hold of Ellie. She loved the thought of doing something different, something other than the normal routine. 'OK then!'

'You'd better get changed,' Joe said, looking at her school uniform. 'You can't go to a horse sale looking like that.'

Ellie quickly shut the door and pulled off the grey polo shirt and black trousers that were her school uniform. She changed back into her jodhpurs and put on a red top and her fleece. As she fixed her hair into a ponytail, her eyes fell on the jewellery box beside her bed. Maybe she should take her money. She might see some things in Barrowton that she could get for her room. She hadn't got any further with her plans for doing it up. She took out the whole lot – three hundred pounds – stuffed it into her purse and ran downstairs.

Ellie had never been to a horse sale before. There were people everywhere, men in flat caps, women with hard faces, a few children. There was the sound of neighing and shouting. Dogs were dashing about through people's legs or being walked on leads. There were two barns and lots of metal pens, all filled with horses and ponies. No one remarked on the fact that Ellie and Joe should be at school.

'That's where they sell the tack,' explained Joe, pointing to the barn on the left. 'The horses and ponies are in the pens over here.'

Ellie walked around, feeling more aware of everything than she had done for a long time. The air felt tense, and full of possibilities, as the horses and ponies were bought and sold.

The pens nearest them held an assortment of shaggy ponies. There were three bay yearlings, an old grey pony, a pretty dark bay mare and a young piebald cob. They all had a card with their sale descriptions on tied to their pen gates. She could feel how confused and anxious they were, the foals huddled together, the other ponies pacing, their eyes scared as people walked past looking at their catalogues and making comments about the horses.

Ellie stopped to stroke the bay mare. In front of them were the pens with the horses in. Her eyes scanned over them – bay, black, skewbald. Then her gaze came to rest on a dirty white-grey horse of about fifteen hands in one of the outer pens. He was an Arab with a dished face, large eyes and delicate muzzle. His mane was long and part of it had rubbed out, his tail was straggling, his ribs prominent. He was in poor condition, but that wasn't the only reason Ellie's gaze fell on him – he was staring straight at her. Ellie had never seen the horse before, ever. But as their eyes met she somehow had the strangest feeling that they had always known each other.

Feeling a bit stupid, she blinked and turned away.

However, even facing the other way, she could still feel the grey horse's eyes on her back, boring into her, insisting she look back at him. She glanced round again. She knew it was mad, but she felt as if he was willing her to go over, and somehow Ellie couldn't refuse. She took a step towards him, but just then Joe touched her arm.

'Let's go to the ring where they are selling the horses.'

Ellie shot one last reluctant look at the skinny grey horse and then followed Joe away.

The sales ring was a large round pen and there was sawdust on the floor. People stood all around it. All Ellie could think about was the grey horse. An auctioneer in a green waistcoat and checked shirt sat on a platform, a small hammer in his hand. A young black gelding of about 16 hands was being trotted round the ring by a man dressed in a brown overall. There was a number stuck to the horse's flank.

'What'll I be bid for lot 113? Three-year-old black gelding, thoroughbred sire. Irish draught mare . . .' The auctioneer's voice came over the loudspeaker.

The people bidding were holding up their hands. Joe pushed through the crowd to find a space right by the bars of the pen, but Ellie hung back. 'I'll just be a moment,' she told Joe. He nodded, absorbed now in the bidding.

Ellie made her way back through the crowds and looked across at the pen where the grey horse was. His back was to her and his head was sagging down. She could almost feel the suffering in the air around him. Suddenly he looked round over his shoulder. It was as though he had sensed she was there.

Almost before she knew it Ellie was hurrying through the crowds towards him, dodging round people, half tripping over dog leads, her eyes on the pen. By the time she reached it, the horse had come to the gate.

She drew in her breath. Closer up, she could see

the full extent of his neglect. His coat was rough and covered with dirt and grass stains. His legs were clogged with mud. There were scars on his knees, shoulder and neck. His ribs stood out. But despite his age and his half-starved condition, there was something about his eyes that captivated her. They were deep and dark and seemed to see right down inside her. She reached out and touched his neck.

A gruff voice spoke behind her. 'That one'll be going to the knackers then.' Ellie glanced over her shoulder. Two men were walking nearby, commenting on the horses in the pens. The man who had spoken was pointing at the grey.

'Not a doubt about it,' said the second man. 'Unwarranted and sold unsound. Look at the state of it.'

'Meat man'll be lucky to get his money's worth with that,' said the first man. He shook his head. 'Poor old sod.' And they walked on. The horse looked at Ellie. Suddenly she was filled with a burning conviction.

'The meat man won't get you,' she said. 'I promise.' She knew she had to buy him. She stroked his neck once more. 'I'll be back in a moment!' And she turned and fled through the crowd.

'You want to do *what*?' Joe stared at her. She dragged him away from the ring.

'I want to buy a horse. How do I do it?'

'But you can't,' Joe protested. 'You haven't got any money.'

'I have. I've got three hundred pounds. It might be enough. He's old and the people I heard talking said no one would want him apart from the meat man.' She stumbled over the horrible words. 'Oh, Joe, I've got to buy him. I can't let that happen.'

'Well, three hundred pounds might be enough,' said Joe, considering it. 'They're not going for much to the meat man these days.' He frowned in concern. 'But you can't just buy a horse, Ellie. Where are you going to keep it? You couldn't take one home, particularly not from a sale. Dad thinks anyone who buys from a sale is a complete halfwit. He'd flip.'

'I don't care!' Ellie declared. 'I'll find somewhere else to keep him. All he needs is a field and a shelter. I've got money I inherited. I bet I'd be allowed to have some of it to keep a horse. In fact, I know I would,' she lied. 'I'm going to do it, Joe. Just tell me how.'

Joe looked very worried. 'Ellie, you can't.'

Ellie glared at him. 'Why not?' She hadn't felt as strongly about anything since her mum and dad . . . No! She stopped herself. *Don't think about them. Not now.*

'You can't just buy a horse,' Joe protested. 'It's mental. It's –' He saw her expression and broke off helplessly. 'I'm not going to change your mind, am I?'

She shook her head. 'Nope.'

Joe took a deep breath. 'OK. So which horse is it?'

Ellie set off through the crowd. 'There!' She pointed at the horse's pen. The horse pricked his ears and looked at her with recognition. 'I told you I'd come back,' Ellie murmured, going over and stroking his cheek. She looked round at Joe to see what he thought.

His jaw had dropped open. 'Ellie! You can't buy that. He's a wreck!'

The horse put his ears back.

Ellie glared at Joe. 'He's not! Well, maybe a bit,' she admitted. 'But that's why he needs my help. I'll make him better.'

'But he's being sold unsound and unwarranted,' Joe said, checking the card. 'That means he's lame and there's probably all sorts of stuff wrong with him, which will mean even if you cure his lameness you won't be able to ride him.'

'I don't care,' Ellie said. This horse was alone in the world, like she was. If she bought him at least they'd have each other. 'I want him.' She turned back to Joe. 'And I'm not going home without him.'

He looked at her stubborn face and groaned.

'And here we have lot 178. A grey gelding, seventeen years old. Sold unwarranted and unsound,' the auctioneer announced as the grey was led into the ring by the man in the brown overalls. The horse walked slowly, his head hanging low, his hooves stumbling on the ground.

The crowd around the ring gave the horse quick dismissive glances and then looked away, chatting among themselves.

The auctioneer glanced over to where a burly man in a hat was standing near the entrance. Joe had told Ellie that was the meat man, buying horses to ship overseas or to go for pet food. He had also warned her that horses were sold in guineas and not pounds, and that he knew she would have to pay taxes and extra things like that on top. 'The highest you can go is two hundred and twenty-five pounds,' he'd warned her.

Ellie clutched her purse in her pocket.

'So what am I bid for this horse?' The auctioneer sounded as if he wanted to get it over and done with as quickly as possible. 'Let's start at two hundred.'

There was no movement in the crowd. Ellie went to stick her hand up, but Joe grabbed it. 'You might get him for less,' he hissed.

'One hundred and fifty then?'

The meat man touched his hat in a bored way. 'One hundred and fifty I'm bid,' said the auctioneer. 'One hundred and fifty. Going . . .'

Joe nudged Ellie and she quickly stuck her hand up.

'We have a bid to the left,' the auctioneer said, clearly surprised. 'That's one hundred and seventy-five to my left.' The meat man touched his hat again. 'Two hundred pounds.'

Ellie raised her hand. 'Two hundred and twenty-five to my left . . .'

Ellie's heart pounded. *Please, please, please don't bid any more*, she silently begged the meat man.

Her heart plummeted as he bid again.

'That's two hundred and fifty.'

'No!' Ellie whispered in despair. 'Joe . . .'

'Bid again,' he told her quickly. 'I've got some money with me.'

She raised her hand.

'That's two hundred and seventy-five to my left . . .'

Ellie looked at the meat man. Relief rushed through her as she saw him give a brief shake of his head.

'Are all bids done? Going, going . . . *gone*!' The auctioneer struck his hammer down.

Ellie swung round. 'Oh, thank you, Joe! Thank you!' She flung her arms round him.

'I can't believe you've actually just bought a horse,' he said, looking at her, almost in awe.

'Neither can I!' she said dazedly.

Just then, one of the officials came over to take Ellie's name and details.

The man told her where to go and pay. Joe gave her some money from his wallet. 'That should be enough. I've got enough left to go and buy him a headcollar and leadrope while you pay.'

Ellie threw him a grateful smile and hurried to the little hut where people paid for the horses. As she waited, the realization of what she had just done began to sink in. What was her uncle going to say? Where was she going to keep the horse? What if the horse needed loads of vet treatment? What if her grandma and the people in charge of her inheritance wouldn't let her have any money to pay for his keep? The adrenaline pumping inside faded and she began to feel sick.

She paid the money over the counter and, holding the receipt in her hands, she walked slowly back to the pen. *Oh God*, she thought over and over again as the reality hit her. *What have I done?*

Joe was standing there. Despite his words from earlier he was stroking the horse's neck and talking quietly to him. The horse's eyes were half closed and he looked as if there was hardly any strength left in him, but as Ellie approached he put his head up and let out a low whinny.

In that instant, Ellie pushed aside all her worries. She broke into a run. 'Hi, boy,' she said as she reached the pen. He nuzzled her hands.

'So what are you going to call him then?' Joe asked.

Ellie thought for a moment. A word came to her. She tried it out in her head.

'You can always name him later, I guess,' Joe went on when she didn't say anything. 'You don't need to name him now and –'

'No, I know what he's called,' Ellie interrupted. She looked at the horse and spoke softly. 'His name's Spirit.'

The horse's eyes met hers.

Ellie opened the gate and went inside the pen. *Spirit.* Her horse. She put her arms round his neck and had the strangest sensation that she had come home.

You're mine, she promised the grey horse silently. *Forever.* She meant it with her whole heart. Whatever the problems, whatever she had to face, Spirit was hers now and she was never ever going to let him go.

Chapter Five

Ellie walked slowly along the country road, with Spirit beside her and Joe on the other side of him.

When Stuart had come to meet them and found out about the horse, his eyebrows had risen almost to the top of his bald head. 'I don't like to think what the boss'll say about this,' he'd said, drawing in a whistling breath through his teeth. But he'd put out his hand and stroked Spirit's muzzle. 'Poor old devil. You've had a hard life by the look of it. What've they done to you?' He glanced at Ellie and she saw the sympathy in his eyes. 'You two hang on here with him and I'll go back and fetch the trailer.'

But when Stuart had returned, Spirit had refused to go anywhere near the trailer. Every time Ellie tried to lead him up the ramp he pulled back violently. When tempting him with food didn't work, Joe and Stuart got behind him to urge him in but he swung his head up, ears flattened, and lashed out with his back feet.

A few jokers from Joe's year who were also bunking off school were standing nearby watching. 'That your new show horse then, Joe?'

'Will you be takin' him in the Horse of the Year show?'

'Bet he'll win *all* the prizes!'

Joe took no notice.

'Maybe it's a present for his new girlfriend.'

'I'd chuck him, love, if that's the best he can do.' They burst out laughing.

'He's my cousin, not my boyfriend!' Ellie retaliated, unable to keep quiet any longer.

'Well then, I'm available!' one of them yelled. 'Why don't you come on over here?'

'Just ignore them,' Joe told her with a sigh. 'They're morons.' He turned to Stuart. 'He's not going in, is he?'

'Let's try the lunge ropes,' Stuart said. He fetched two lunge reins from the front and explained to Ellie what he was going to do. 'We'll fasten them on to the box, Joe'll take one and I'll have the other, we'll bring them round behind him and see if that gets him going forward into the trailer.'

Ellie shot a doubtful look at Spirit. His head was up and he was looking at Stuart and the ropes suspiciously. 'Isn't there anything else we can do?' She had a very strong feeling this wasn't going to work.

'Let's give it a go.' Stuart laid a hand on Spirit's

neck, his voice gentle. 'Come on, lad. Let's get you in the box and take you home.'

He clipped the ropes on to rings at the side of the entrance to the ramp. Ellie then led Spirit forward, while Joe and Stuart went behind the horse and brought the lunge reins up so they crossed over and touched his tail. Ellie felt Spirit stiffen and his ears flicked backwards.

'This isn't going to –'

Spirit reared straight up as the lunge reins tightened against him. His front hooves lashed in the air, narrowly missing Ellie's head. His eyes, which had been so empty, suddenly flashed with a long-lost defiance. As he came down, he leapt forwards, almost pulling Ellie off her feet. The new leadrope burnt through her hands, but she hung on tightly as he plunged around her.

'Steady, boy, steady!' she cried.

The boys watching jeered.

'Whoa! Rodeo horse!'

'Hold him, cowgirl!'

Spirit came to a stop and she stroked his neck, trying to block out the calls. 'It's OK,' she soothed the horse. 'It's OK.'

'Are you all right?' Joe demanded, reaching her.

She nodded.

'Let's try again,' Stuart said, coming over.

But Ellie shook her head. 'It isn't going to work,'

she said, her hand on the horse's neck, her eyes on his. She knew, as clearly as if she could read his mind, that there was no way he would go into the trailer that day. 'I'll walk him home.'

Stuart and Joe had tried to argue with her, but in the end they had finally agreed it might be the most sensible thing to do. Now Ellie and Joe walked Spirit along the road that led up from the town in the valley. The empty fields stretched out on either side of them, rising up to the high peaks. A bitter wind blew down the mountainsides, shaking the strands of barbed wire above the stone walls. Everywhere looked so desolate. Ellie shivered, wishing she had some gloves with her. Her fingers were freezing. She put one hand on Spirit's neck, tucking it under his mane and feeling the warmth from his skin seep into her. The horse's head was stretched out low and he was stumbling every few steps as he walked. 'Looks like he's lame in his near shoulder,' said Joe, breaking the silence.

Ellie nodded. She'd noticed that, and also the scars on his shoulder and legs. How had he got those? His mane and tail were matted and full of burrs, and his coat was thick with grease and dirt, standing out dully from his skin. He was skinny, and his neck was weak and un-muscled. He was a far cry from her uncle's glossy, fit animals.

As she thought about her uncle, she felt slightly ill again. She'd been full of bravado at the sale, but now they were getting close her nerves were starting to build. What if he wouldn't let her keep Spirit at the stables? He wasn't the type of man who would be persuaded into anything and he certainly wouldn't let her keep Spirit out of the kindness of his heart. *Then I'll keep him somewhere else*, she told herself firmly. *Gran said I've got lots of money in trust. I'll just use some of that. Gran and the other people* have *to let me.*

But what if they didn't?

But Ellie knew she couldn't let herself think like that. She stroked Spirit's neck. Whatever happened she wasn't going to let him go. As if he sensed her thoughts, Spirit raised his head and looked at her. Ellie smiled. *You're mine*, she told him in her head. *I'll find a way to keep you. I promise.*

Just then, there was the sound of an engine. 'It's Luke,' Joe said as a motorbike came down the hill from the direction of the stables.

Ellie felt her insides tighten. Luke stopped a little way off and cut the engine. Getting off his bike and tucking his helmet under his arm, he walked down the road towards them in his black leather motorcycling gear, his dark hair falling across his forehead.

'Oh my God!' He shook his head in disbelief as he reached them. 'Stuart told me what you'd done but . . . oh my God! Len's seriously going to freak.' His eyes swept to Ellie, an amused, incredulous smile twitching at his lips. 'Have you got a death wish or something? I mean, buying any horse without his say would make him mad, but to get a knackered horse like that –'

'He's not knackered!' Ellie responded, stroking Spirit's neck protectively. 'He's been ill-treated. He'll be fine. He just needs love and care.'

'So will you after Len's finished with you!' Luke turned to Joe. 'I can't believe you let her do it.'

'Yeah, well, she's not that easy to stop,' Joe said glumly.

Ellie was too busy stroking Spirit to bother getting cross with them for talking about her. Luke's gaze flicked back to her face, a new assessing look in his eyes. 'You know something, you're turning into good value to have around, Ellie. I'll give you that.'

Ellie frowned. 'Oh, shut up. It's not that big a deal. I've got money. I'll pay for Spirit's keep or keep him somewhere else if Uncle Len won't let me keep him at the stables. It'll be fine.'

Luke raised his eyebrows. 'I'll remind you of that. Good luck with it then. I'll see you later – if you're still alive, of course.' He strode back to his bike. Ellie clicked her tongue and walked Spirit on. The horse stumbled and Luke chuckled as he straddled the bike, blue eyes glinting. 'Look on the bright side. Maybe the old nag'll drop dead by the time you get him home and Len will never need to know about him.'

'He's not an old nag!' Ellie yelled furiously as she pulled Spirit past. A few minutes later, she heard the roar of the bike as it started up and Luke headed away.

'He is *so* annoying,' she complained for about the millionth time to Joe.

'Forget Luke,' Joe said drily. 'You should be thinking about what you'll say to Dad.'

Len wasn't due back until feedtime. Ellie tied Spirit up outside and went in to phone her grandma.

It was very early in the morning in New Zealand and her gran sounded half asleep. 'What is it, sweetheart? Is everything OK?' she asked, as in the kitchen Pip jumped around Ellie's legs, putting her paws up on Ellie's knees.

Ellie could heard the alarm in her gran's voice. 'It's fine. It's just I really need to speak to you, Gran,' she said, fondling the little dog's head. She hadn't wanted to wake her gran up, but she knew she had to talk to her before Len came back. 'Um, the thing is I . . . well, I've just bought a horse and I was hoping, well, can I have the money to keep him?'

There was silence. Ellie held her breath and crossed her fingers. *Please, please, please*, she prayed.

'Oh!' her gran said. She gave an astonished laugh. 'Oh, goodness, Ellie. You're so like your mum at times. So you've just bought a horse! What does your uncle think?'

'Um, he's OK with it,' Ellie lied.

'Well then, sure, I guess. You can have the money for the horse's keep. I know your mum and dad would have been happy for you to have one. I'll talk to the executors of the will, but yes, I'm sure it can be arranged.'

After saying their goodbyes, Ellie clicked the phone off, feeling a massive rush of relief. Phew. One obstacle down. Now there was just her uncle to face – but she didn't want to think about that. Pushing the thought to the back of her mind, she picked up Pip and gave the little dog a cuddle. 'Luke'll be back soon, though it beats me why you like him so much.'

Pip wriggled and licked her nose.

Ellie went outside. Stuart suggested she put Spirit in one of the foaling boxes round the back that were not in use. They were large roomy stables, well away from the other horses. Ellie bedded one of the stables down with a thick layer of golden straw, and filled a haynet and a water bucket. Then she fetched Spirit. He hesitated as she tried to lead him in, stopping a few metres away.

'Come on, boy.' Ellie clicked her tongue and pulled on the leadrope, but looking at his face she could see that he was worried. His ears were flicking back and forward and his head was up.

'OK. Well, there's no rush,' she told him. She loosened the leadrope and stood quietly beside him, stroking his neck until the tension left him and he pushed against her with his nose. She fed him a mint from her pocket and then rubbed his forehead. 'I promise it'll be all right. Look. I'll go in.' Putting the leadrope over his neck, she walked into the stable and came back out. 'See, it's all right.' She patted his neck and then walked into the stable again. This time, Spirit followed her inside, his head stretching out, so his muzzle just touched the small of her back.

Ellie felt a wave of love as she saw the trust in his eyes. 'There,' she said, taking the headcollar off. He walked around, sniffing the straw and snorting, his eyes wide, as if he could hardly believe it. Ravenously, he pulled out a big mouthful of sweet hay from the haynet. Ellie smoothed down his mane and straightened his forelock. She was longing to start grooming him – to get rid of the grass stains and mud, the tangles and burrs – but some part of her sensed that she needed to be patient and give the horse time to adjust and settle in. She wished she knew all about him, where he had come from, why he was in such bad condition. She could guess that bad things must have happened to him from the scars left on him and the fact he was so nervous of horseboxes and stables.

'You're safe now, though,' she murmured, and for

the next hour she just stayed in the stable with him, stroking him and keeping him company.

At feedtime her uncle arrived home. 'He's here,' Joe said, coming to Spirit's stable door.

Ellie knew it. She had heard the car arrive.

'Look, I'll come with you,' Joe went on worriedly. 'Help you explain.'

But Ellie remembered what had happened the last time Joe had tried to help her. 'No.' She swallowed. 'It's OK. I'll tell him on my own.'

She readied herself to confront her uncle, feeling as if she was about to walk into a lion's cage. But as she reached the door of the stable she heard a soft whicker. She looked round and saw Spirit staring at her. 'I'll be back soon,' she reassured him.

She went up the yard, her heart beating fast. Part of her wanted to run away, to hide, to wait until her uncle found out, but she also knew she had to face the music some time. There was no point putting it off. She might as well just get it over with.

Her uncle was in the kitchen. Ellie put her hand on the door handle and, squaring her shoulders, walked inside.

Chapter Six

Len spoke slowly, as if trying to understand the words. 'You've bought a horse?' His eyes hardened to flint. 'At the market? You bought a horse at the market this morning?'

Ellie nodded. 'I had some money that Gran had given me. I phoned her and she said I can keep him.'

'*She* said?' Len's voice rose angrily. 'She's the other side of the bloody world! Well, it can't stay. You'll have to sell it.' He marched towards the door.

Fear gave Ellie courage. She jumped in front of him. 'No. I won't.'

'You won't?' Len stared at her. 'You'll do as I say, lass.'

'No!' Ellie said desperately, her heart pounding. 'I'm not taking him back to the sale!'

Len slammed his fist into the table. 'You will do what I damn well say!' he roared.

Adrenaline coursed through Ellie. 'I won't! I'm keeping him! If you won't let me keep him here, then fine, I'll keep him somewhere else. But Gran said I could have a horse. She said I could have the money!'

They glared at each other.

When Len spoke, his voice was dangerously soft. 'So, when you had this conversation with your gran, you told her that you'd picked this horse up from a sale, did you? You told her that he was unwarranted and unsound, which he must have been if you could afford him?'

Ellie didn't answer.

'He *was* unwarranted, wasn't he?'

Ellie nodded.

'And unsound?' Len pressed on.

Ellie had no choice but to nod again.

'And you think when I tell your gran this, it won't make her change her mind?'

Ellie knew he had her. If he told her gran that, she knew just what the reaction would be. Spirit would be sold, no arguing. Her shoulders sagged, the fight going out of her. 'Please,' she said desperately. 'Please, Uncle Len, let me keep him. Gran said I can pay for his food and stabling. He won't cost you and I'll do anything. I'll . . .' A thought struck her. It would mean backing down, which she hated, but she'd do it for Spirit. 'I'll ride the ponies for you,' she offered quickly. 'Whenever you want. At shows or here, and I'll work really hard on the yard.'

Len's eyes narrowed. 'You're suggesting we do a deal?'

'Yes.' Ellie thought he was going to explode again, but to her surprise his forehead furrowed.

'Well, I do need a rider for the smaller ponies.' Len considered her for a moment and then gave a curt nod. 'All right. But on *my* terms . . .'

Ellie caught her breath in relief.

'He's only here on a temporary basis. I don't have room on this yard for pets and the time you spend with him will be time you could be with the others, working them. You can keep him for six weeks. Get some condition on him and then sell him on. Maybe make yourself a few bob. You've got him now so it makes sense.'

Ellie hesitated. She had absolutely no intention of ever selling Spirit on and trying to make money out of him, but she could see that telling her uncle this would get her nowhere right now. At least he was agreeing that she could keep the horse. That was enough. She'd deal with the selling part of the deal later. She nodded. 'Thank you.'

'Let's see him then,' her uncle grunted. 'See what sort of eye for a horse you've got. Maybe, just maybe, you've got yourself a bargain.'

He opened the door and Ellie followed him back outside, feeling nervous. What was he going to say when he saw Spirit? Joe was standing by the water

78

trough, pretending to scrub out a bucket. His eyes flew to Ellie's face. She nodded quickly, trying to let him know it was OK. She took her uncle to the foaling box where Spirit was.

'This is him, this is Spirit.'

As Len joined her at the door, Spirit shied back in alarm. He stood at the back of the box, head high, body trembling. Ellie saw him through her uncle's eyes – his ribs standing out like a toast rack, his dull coat, his scarred legs and shoulder.

'Oh, flamin' heck.' Len groaned. He shook his head and Ellie saw the bitter disappointment in his gaze. 'Well, you won't be getting your money back on that. Best you can hope for is to get a bit more meat on his bones and sell him to the knackers for a better price.' He glanced down at her. 'Still, a deal's a deal. You ride the ponies, you get to keep him for six weeks.'

'How much shall I pay you?' Ellie could hardly quite believe it.

'You can have his stabling and feed in exchange for riding for me. Vets and farrier bills, you pay.' Len turned away. 'Oh, and by the way,' he shot over his shoulder, 'you're grounded for skipping school.'

Ellie didn't care about being grounded. She never went out anyway, only ever spending time with Joe or on the yard, and all she wanted now was to be with Spirit, feeding him up, grooming him, looking after him. That night she went out straight after supper. There was a strong wind blowing and she had to fight her way across the yard, the gusts buffeting her, whipping her breath away as she walked. But inside Spirit's stable it was warm and peaceful. Sweep, who had left the barn now, had found the new straw bed Ellie had put down and was curled up contentedly in the corner under the manger, while Spirit pulled at his haynet hung on the back wall, unbothered by the kitten's presence. He jumped anxiously as she slid the bolts back, but relaxed and whickered softly when he realized it was her.

'Hey, boy.' Ellie had brushed the worst of the mud off his coat after feedtime and put on a rug to keep him warm. He pushed his nose into her chest. She smoothed down his forelock, sending out waves of love. He might not look like anything now but he would soon look better. 'I'll make you well,' she promised him. 'And I'll never sell you on, no matter what Uncle Len says.'

Spirit snorted and then moved back to his haynet.

Ellie sat down in the corner of the stall on the straw next to Sweep. Wrapping her arms round her knees, she imagined Spirit fit and healthy, the fear gone from his eyes. Every bit of stubbornness inside her felt like it was focused into a fierce determination. She would do it. She *would* make him better.

When the alarm clock went off the next morning, Ellie blinked her eyes open and a single thought filled her head. *Spirit*. She sat up in bed as the events of the day before came rushing back. She caught her breath. It had all really happened.

Jumping up, she pulled on her clothes and ran down the stairs, hair unbrushed. As she burst out of the door into the dark winter morning, a few horses heard her and whickered hopefully, thinking it was breakfast time. Ellie took no notice. She raced to Spirit's stable. He jumped nervously as she opened the door, but then his nostrils quivered in a nicker and he stepped towards her, moving like a ghost through the dim light. Ellie felt like throwing her arms round his neck but she didn't want to startle him. Restraining the impulse, she made herself wait until he reached her and then she gently touched his face.

'You're real,' she whispered in delight. 'Oh, Spirit. You're real!' He lifted his muzzle to her face, blowing out. She breathed in and then gently breathed back. Her mum had told her it was the way horses greeted each other.

Spirit's rug had slipped slightly in the night, so she straightened that and then refilled his water bucket and kicked the straw back from the door. She'd muck him out later after feeding. She was going to be on the yard all day because there was a teacher-training day at school. 'I'll start grooming you later this morning,' she promised him. 'I'm going to make you look beautiful.'

But her uncle had other plans. When she heard him come on to the yard with Luke and Joe, she went to help them with giving out the feeds. Len pointed at her. 'I want you in the ring with Luke and Joe at nine o'clock. You can ride Merlin to start.'

Ellie bit back the desire to argue. She couldn't afford to annoy her uncle now. Instead she nodded.

He strode away and started dealing out the buckets of feed.

Just before nine, Ellie led Merlin into the ring and mounted up. His bay coat had been quick to groom and he had seemed to enjoy the attention. Luke was to ride Gabriel and Joe would be on Picasso. Gabriel was calm, but Picasso was fidgeting, moving constantly, staring in all directions.

'Merlin will look after you,' Joe said to Ellie as he fastened Picasso's girth and only narrowly avoided the pony stepping on his feet. 'Not like this nutter.' He patted Picasso's neck as he said it, and swung quickly into the saddle. Picasso leapt forwards but Joe moved with him, pulling him up and getting him back under control. 'Come on,' he said, touching the pony with his heels. 'Let's get you working in.' Picasso walked off with quick short strides.

Luke had already mounted Gabriel and was trotting round on a loose rein. Pip was sitting at the side of the ring, her eyes never leaving him, her pink tongue hanging out.

Ellie checked her girth and mounted. It was four months since she had last ridden but it didn't feel strange at all. If she was honest, it felt like coming home.

She walked Merlin on. For a small pony, he had a long stride and was very well schooled. He didn't ever go faster than he needed to, but he was obedient to Ellie's aids and when she asked him to trot and canter he obliged cheerfully. By the time Len came into the school, she was trotting and cantering circles.

He strode into the middle and watched her for a few moments. 'Looks like you can sit on a horse, anyway,' he commented.

From having watched him coaching Luke and Joe the past few weeks, Ellie knew that was about the most of a compliment she could expect. Still, at least it was better than him criticizing. She patted Merlin's solid neck.

Len got them all riding round together. It was basic stuff – circles in walk, trot and canter, transitions through all three paces, serpentines and loops. Ellie had done everything before in lessons with other teachers, but she had never known anyone as demanding as Len. Every circle had to be perfectly round, every transition dead on the marker. But she was determined to get it right. It wasn't in her nature to do anything half-heartedly, and even though she disliked her uncle she was going to meet her half of the deal. After all, Spirit was at stake.

Ellie found that when she was riding it helped to try to see her uncle just as a riding coach. Although he was tough to please, it was clear that he knew a lot and her own desire to prove her ability pushed to the fore. She concentrated hard and felt a determined sort of pride whenever she got a rare word of praise.

'Turn in and halt!' Len called to them all at last. He looked at Ellie. 'You ride well. Let's have you off that old pony and on to Picasso. Joe, take Merlin in and bring out Barney. We'll do some jumping.'

Picasso! Ellie glanced at Joe to see if he minded having to change ponies, but he didn't look bothered. As she dismounted and they swapped, he smiled. 'You're doing brilliantly.'

'Thanks.' Ellie took Picasso's reins. 'Any tips?'

'Sit deep,' warned Joe. 'He's got a big jump on him and he might throw in a buck or two the first few times over a fence. He's not like Merlin – you'll need to watch out for yourself. See you in a minute.' He led Merlin out, and Ellie adjusted the stirrups and then mounted Picasso. He felt totally different to ride. Now Joe had ridden him in he had settled down, but it still took only the slightest touch of her legs to make him increase his speed. He pulled at the bit. She kept her contact light, riding him forward but not letting him go too fast. The first time round the ring he tested her out, shying away from the fence and shooting towards the gate, but she sat deep as Joe had said and within seconds had him back on the track at the side of the ring. She patted his neck as she rode him round at a brisk trot. He felt like a mini-racehorse, bristling with energy.

Len was putting out some jumps. He set out a grid of three low fences, with a stride between each one. 'All right then. Off you go, Luke. Take it at a trot.'

Luke trotted Gabriel round, the usual careless look in his blue eyes replaced by an intense concentration. Gabriel tried to speed up but Luke sat deep in the saddle, his long legs wrapping round the horse as he slowed him down instantly. The bay horse responded and trotted over the jumps, taking them easily in his stride, with Luke light in the saddle. Luke patted his neck. Then it was Ellie's turn. She could feel her breath shorten with excitement. She loved jumping. She wished she could canter, but she held Picasso back at a trot as her uncle had instructed, even though, like Gabriel, Picasso tried to rush. At the last moment she freed his head and they bounced easily over all three jumps. She was glad Joe had given her a warning about sitting deep. As they landed over the final one, Picasso put his head between his knees and bucked. She was ready for him and sat down hard, pulling his head up and turning him in a circle before he could try again.

An uncharacteristic smile briefly touched Len's face. 'Well sat. Bring him round again.'

As Ellie rode past Luke, she saw that he was grinning. 'Thought he was going to have you off there.'

Yeah, and then wouldn't you have laughed, thought Ellie. But actually she was enjoying the ride too much to feel annoyed by Luke.

Len had her go round two more times at a trot before letting her canter over the fences, and then he changed the distance. 'One stride at the first and second, two at the third now. Get them listening.'

And so the lesson went on. After warming Barney up at the far end of the ring, Joe joined in.

After a while, Len got them to halt and then took one jump out and raised the poles on the others to well over four feet. They looked very large. 'Don't worry,' Joe said, glancing at Ellie. 'This won't be for us to jump. This'll be for Luke. Dad won't risk the ponies' legs jumping that high.' He patted Barney's neck. The mischief in Barney gave him a wonderful merriness when he was being ridden. Ellie wondered when she would get to ride him.

Suddenly the deal she had struck with her uncle didn't seem quite so bad. She'd always loved going in shows on Abbey. Now she was riding for her uncle, would she get to ride Picasso or Barney, or maybe some of the novices in showing classes for him?

Ellie watched as Luke cantered Gabriel round, getting him steady and ready to jump. Although the fences were big, Luke didn't show a flicker of nerves. He cantered the horse towards the fences, effortlessly found the right place to jump from, and Gabriel soared over them.

'Well done!' Ellie called impulsively as Luke clapped a hand on the horse's neck and cantered easily back to her and Joe.

Luke pulled Gabriel to a halt. 'Fancy a go?' he challenged.

Ellie met his stare. 'Why not?'

Her uncle's voice broke in. 'Not a bad idea. Let's see what you can do. Hop up on Gabriel and have a try.'

Ellie saw Luke's face register astonishment. She swung round and looked at her uncle at the same time as Joe protested beside her.

'Dad! You can't get Ellie to jump four and a half foot on a strange horse.'

'I'll be the judge of that!' Len gave Ellie an appraising look. 'Come on then.'

For a moment Ellie hesitated and then nodded. 'Sure,' she said coolly, throwing her leg over Picasso's saddle and jumping off.

She caught a flicker of surprise on her uncle's face, and in that instant realized he'd been expecting her to refuse. The knowledge fired her up and she handed Picasso's reins to Joe. It was a bigger jump than she had ever done before and she'd never ridden Gabriel, but she'd do it.

'Ellie, you can say no,' Joe whispered quickly, shooting a look at Len who had gone to stomp down some of the rough surface in front of the jump.

'Don't listen to him,' Luke said, sliding off Gabriel. 'Go on. Do it.' An amused smile curled at the corners of his mouth.

'Ellie, don't be stupid,' Joe said in a low voice. 'At least ask Dad to put it down.'

But pride and adrenaline were surging through her. 'I'll be OK.'

She took the reins from Luke and mounted. After Picasso, Gabriel felt very big. Len was back in the middle now, watching her shrewdly, arms folded as she quickly adjusted her stirrups, checked her girth and then rode off. She concentrated on the horse's long stride, trying to force her nervousness down. She could see from her uncle's face that he was still expecting her to pull out. Luke probably was too. But that just made her even more determined – there was no way she was going to give either of them the satisfaction. *Just watch this*, she thought.

'Now?' she called, glancing across at Len.

He nodded. Ellie clicked her tongue and felt Gabriel surge into a canter. He might be big but he was obedient and, despite his size, he felt easier to ride than Picasso. Ellie remembered all her mum had ever taught her about jumping. Ride at the middle of the fence, look up, keep your legs on. Fear spiked through her for a moment. She'd jumped Abbey lots but this was different.

You can do it, she told herself. *You can.*

She turned the corner. As Gabriel saw the jump, his ears pricked and he increased his speed. 'Steady, boy,' Ellie murmured, taking a firmer hold on the reins. He'd been well schooled by Luke and he came back to hand straight away. The jump loomed up, massive, solid, mountain-like. Suddenly the fear faded. She saw where they needed to take off. She pushed Gabriel on, lengthening his stride to hit the spot. *One, two, three . . .*

And they were over!

But Ellie didn't have time to even think. The next fence was right in front of them. She sat down in the saddle and pushed on again. *One stride. Two strides and up . . .*

They soared through the air. As Gabriel landed cleanly and cantered on round the school, the breath left Ellie in a rush. Her adrenaline faded and she felt her legs get suddenly shaky, but she'd done it! Trying not to grin like an insane Cheshire cat, she slowed Gabriel down and looked triumphantly at her uncle.

'Not bad, lass,' he said and smiled approvingly.

Ellie rode Gabriel up to join the others. Joe looked very relieved. 'That was brilliant. You were awesome!'

I did it, I did it! the words sang inside her head.

'Right, Picasso and Gabriel have done enough. Swap back and take them out for fifteen minutes on the lanes,' Len told them. 'Joe, you stay in here. Barney can do a bit more.'

Ellie and Luke rode out of the school, through the courtyard and down the bumpy lane, letting the horses walk out on a loose rein to cool them down.

'You're a dark horse then,' Luke said, glancing across at Ellie. 'I thought you must be scared to ride when you created so much fuss about riding the ponies.'

Ellie shrugged and looked down at Picasso's mane. 'Yeah, well, you thought wrong.'

She was pleased that Luke seemed to be looking at her with new eyes, but it still didn't mean that she wanted to be his friend. She wasn't prepared to forget the kittens or his arrogant behaviour, or his comments about Spirit.

She could feel his eyes on her for a long moment, and then he laughed and got out his phone. The next minute he had started texting one-handed, completely unconcerned.

Ellie ignored him and concentrated on Picasso's neck, stroking his mane.

She and Luke got back to the yard without exchanging another word.

Chapter Seven

Ellie was kept busy all morning. Her uncle told her to ride Milly and then Gem. Milly was bouncy, eager for action, a roller coaster of a pony. Gem was quieter and needed a lot of reassurance and encouragement, his eyes as wide as Bambi's as he stared cautiously around the ring, seeing ghosts everywhere. As Ellie put their tack away, she thought how much more purpose her day seemed to have now she had Spirit and was riding the ponies.

Before Stuart had his lunch, he watched as Ellie trotted Spirit out and confirmed what Joe had thought – that Spirit was lame in his left shoulder. 'It's probably the result of a fall or a knock. Let's rest him for the week and then see how he is. If he's still no better, then we'll call the vet. But maybe it'll right itself.'

'What about his tendons?' Ellie asked. She'd noticed they were slightly swollen.

'Try poulticing them for a few days. There's some

kaolin in the first aid cupboard. Do you know what to do?'

Ellie nodded. Her dad had shown her how to poultice legs two years ago. She saw him in her mind's eye – his dark head by the horse's leg, looking up as he gave her instructions – and she felt grief flood through her again. She fought it down, her hand methodically stroking Spirit's neck, trying to hide her feelings. Spirit pushed against her gently with his nose as if sensing her unhappiness. She swallowed, focusing on him, forcing away the pain.

'Apart from that, he just needs some good feeding,' Stuart went on, shaking his bald head. 'There's more fat on a chip than on him. I'll sort him out some boiled barley and linseed jelly. Plenty of good hay should help too.'

'Thanks, Stuart.' Ellie was grateful. Stuart could have been just as dismissive as her uncle, but he seemed keen to help Spirit and make him better.

Taking Spirit back to his stable, she set to work grooming him. He was calmer now than he had been and let her groom him. She brushed his coat with a dandy brush and then detangled his mane and tail, pulling out the burrs as gently as she could. After that, she started on the hard work of grooming him with a body brush and curry comb.

Spirit lowered his head as she pushed the brush over his coat again and again, cleaning the bristles every few strokes. It was quiet and peaceful in the stable and Ellie lost herself in the rhythm, letting the silence sit comfortably around them. When she had finished brushing his body, she ran her hands down his legs, checking out the lumps and bumps.

Suddenly the stable bolt was pulled back. Spirit started in alarm, pulling the leadrope tight, his head shooting up.

Ellie jumped to her feet. 'Steady!'

'Sorry,' Joe apologized from the door. 'I didn't mean to startle him.'

'Hush now,' Ellie soothed Spirit, stroking his neck. 'It's only Joe.' She glanced over her shoulder. 'It's OK. He's just really jumpy. Something must have happened to him in the past.'

Joe came into the stable and stood by the door, near enough for Spirit to touch him if he wanted to, but not forcing his presence on the tense horse.

After a few minutes Spirit relaxed and nuzzled at Joe's pockets, scenting the Polos that Joe carried at all times. His head lifted warily as Joe went to pat him but he didn't move back, staying where he was to let Joe stroke his now clean neck and feed him a Polo.

'It's weird how he's nervous of everyone but you.'

Ellie nodded. She couldn't explain it but she still had that feeling she'd had at the horse sale that she and Spirit somehow belonged together. She'd never felt anything like it with any other animal even though she'd loved Abbey to bits. It was the strangest, strongest feeling ever.

'I think you were amazing to buy him and face Dad,' Joe went on, watching them. 'I hope Spirit gets over his lameness so you can ride him.'

'He will,' said Ellie with conviction.

Joe looked worried. 'But then Dad will make you sell him.'

Ellie's mouth set in a mutinous line, but before she could say anything there was the sound of the grooms coming back on to the yard. They should get on with some work; the last thing she wanted was to get into her uncle's bad books. 'We'd better go.'

Spirit whickered, his eyes watching her as she left the stable.

The afternoon was filled with grooming and tack cleaning, and Joe and Ellie had to get Barney and two of the other ponies ready for a winter show the next day. Ellie had hardly any time with Spirit, but as soon as supper was finished she went back outside.

The moon was full overhead, casting a silvery glow over the yard as Ellie hurried to Spirit's stable. As she pulled back the bolts, he stiffened. Ellie murmured reassuringly, wondering again about his life before she had bought him. What had happened to him? Why was he scared of the stable door opening?

Where had his scars come from? If only she knew, then maybe she could help him recover.

As she patted Spirit, she hoped he could feel how much she loved him and wanted to help. *You're safe now*, she told him silently. *I promise nothing bad's ever going to happen to you again.*

She shut her eyes and lost herself in the feeling of being with Spirit. Her mind emptied, everything else fading away. It was a blissful feeling – to think nothing, feel nothing, just to focus on him.

Both of them jumped when Joe's voice broke softly through the silence. 'Ellie?'

Ellie turned. Joe was at the stable door. She blinked, feeling disorientated, not knowing how long she had been standing there.

'Are you OK? I was worried about you. It's getting late.'

'I'm coming in now.' Ellie rubbed Spirit's nose and he pushed against her. 'Night, boy.' He whickered softly, and as she stepped out of the stable the world seemed slightly unreal, as if she had been somewhere else for a while.

'What were you doing?' Joe asked as they began walking back to the house together, sending the yard cats scattering in the moonlight.

Ellie shrugged. 'Just being with him.'

Joe shot her a sideways look but seemed to understand.

She sighed. 'I want to help him so much. I wish I knew what had happened to him – why he's so nervous. It might help.'

'Pity there wasn't more information with him at the sale,' Joe said.

Ellie nodded.

They reached the house. 'So, what are you going to do now?' he asked. 'Watch TV or go to your room?'

'Not sure. What about you?'

'I should do some revision, but it's Friday night and I can't face it. Do you want to listen to some music?'

'Cool.' Joe had been lending her CDs and downloading tracks on to her iPod ever since she'd arrived. *Educating her*, as he put it, telling her about British bands while she introduced him to just as many new bands from New Zealand and Australia.

For the rest of the evening they sat in his room, Ellie on the bed and Joe sitting on the floor, playing occasionally on his electric guitar but without it plugged in. He was only allowed to play it properly when Len was out of the house.

'Here!' Joe said, stabbing his finger in the air as they listened to a track he'd downloaded. 'Just listen to the guitar break – the Black Squares are going to be mega.'

Ellie laughed and rolled her eyes. 'They sound like every other new British band.'

'I don't *think* so,' Joe retorted. 'Just use your ears

and listen. I wish they'd do a gig up here, then you'd see how good they are.'

'Not convinced. The Giraffes are loads better.'

'The Giraffes? That band you played me last week? No way!'

The conversation went on like this until Ellie heard Len walk to his room and go to bed. Glancing at the clock, she saw that it was past eleven. Luke was still out in town.

'I'd better go to bed,' she said.

Joe lifted his hand from where he was sitting. 'See you in the morning.'

Ellie smiled and slipped out of his room, making her way up to the next floor. There was a strange feeling inside her. She puzzled about it for a few moments.

I feel . . . *happy*.

As soon as she'd recognized it, the feeling faded to be replaced with an instant guilt. How could she feel happy when her parents were dead? But even though a part of Ellie wanted to deny it, she knew the happiness had been there, if only fleetingly, and she also knew that her parents would have wanted her to be happy again.

For the first time since she'd arrived, when she went to bed that night she curled up under her duvet and didn't cry.

Chapter Eight

Len and Joe headed off to the winter horse show early in the morning. None of the horses and ponies Luke usually rode were entered for the show – Joe had explained to Ellie that showing campaigns were planned carefully so that each horse and pony wasn't taken to too many shows in case they got bored and lost their sparkle in the ring. Along with Barney in the horsebox that day were Fizz and Bill, two ponies who Len produced for his client Veronica Armstrong.

It was very peaceful on the yard without Len around. Ellie followed the instructions on the board and schooled Milly, before riding out on Gem and then riding Wisp, a young show hunter pony, in the school. Luke was riding at the same time but they pretty much ignored each other.

Whenever Ellie could, she stopped by to see Spirit. He was still very nervous, pacing back and forwards in his stable anxiously, only stopping when Ellie was standing with him.

'It's OK,' she told him at lunchtime. 'Really it is. There's no need to be scared now you're here.'

But though her presence soothed him, her words couldn't seem to reach him.

He'll calm down soon, Ellie told herself. *He just needs time.*

When Len drove the horsebox back that afternoon, it turned out that the team had had a good day. Barney had won his open working hunter pony class and the other two ponies had both been placed.

'It'll be your turn soon, lass,' Len said to Ellie as she helped unload the ponies. His eyes narrowed as he gave her a speculative look. 'Picasso's entered for a show tomorrow in Preston which Joe will take him in but then, in a few weeks' time, you can start competing him. There's a big show mid-March with one of the first Royal International qualifiers. I'll enter you for that.'

Ellie nodded as if it was no big deal, but inside she felt a rush of excitement. So she *would* be going in shows. She'd only ever ridden Abbey in jumping classes, gymkhana games and a few Pony Club novice dressage tests before. Going in a working hunter pony class at a big show would be a completely different experience. She thought about the pictures she had seen in her uncle's magazines of champions being presented with sashes and rosettes, and realized that could be her and Picasso in just a few weeks. *I'm going to practise as much as I can*, she decided.

But things didn't go according to plan. The next day Joe and Len set off in the horsebox, with Picasso plaited, groomed and rugged up. His tail bandage was on neatly and his travel boots were carefully fastened. However, half an hour later, the horsebox came back down the lane. Ellie could hear frantic kicking from inside, hooves slamming into wood with crashes and thuds.

She went down to the car park, wondering what was going on. As soon as her uncle got out, she saw how angry he was. He marched round to the ramp and let it down quickly.

'Stupid flamin' pony!' he said, going up the ramp and swinging the partition across. For a second Ellie saw Picasso inside, rug askew and tail bandage in a heap on the floor, and then the pony reared up, snapping the bale string he was tied to and shooting down the ramp, only just avoiding Len. Joe jumped down from the passenger side and made a grab for him, but Picasso shied round him and cantered up to the yard with Joe chasing after him.

Len stood staring at the damaged inside of the horsebox, lips pursed. The inside partition had been kicked to pieces. The leather padding was torn and there was a hole through it.

Ellie knew better than to approach her uncle when he looked like that. She went back on to the yard and found Joe holding Picasso while Stuart checked the pony's legs over for injuries. There was a slight cut just above one of his hind hooves, but otherwise the padded travel boots seemed to have protected him well.

'What happened?' said Ellie, stroking the pony's lathered neck. She could feel the tension in his muscles, feel the stress radiating off him.

Joe looked mystified. 'I've no idea. We were just driving along and Picasso flipped. Dad stopped and I went to see what the matter was. Picasso was bucking and kicking like a crazy thing. We couldn't calm him down and so just had to bring him back. There was no reason for it. He's never liked travelling much, but he's never done anything like that before. Dad's mad about it. It'll cost a fortune to repair the box.'

'Is Picasso OK?' Ellie asked Stuart.

Stuart nodded. 'Seems to be. Take him down to the trough and hose that cut, Joe. Ten minutes of cold water should help keep the swelling down.'

Luckily, Picasso's cut healed quickly and he was only off work for a couple of days. Len sent off an entry for the qualifying show in mid-March with Ellie named as Picasso's rider. Ellie was worried what Joe would think about her riding Picasso, but he seemed supremely unbothered when she asked him if it was OK.

'Definitely. I'm too tall for Picasso now anyway and like I told you, I don't like shows. I do them because I have to, that's all,' Joe said. 'If you take Picasso in, it saves me from a class. You're doing me a favour.'

Ellie could hardly believe he really felt like that. Going to a show seemed so exciting, but Joe genuinely didn't appear to enjoy it.

On Wednesday Len took her to a saddlers where she was kitted out with a showing outfit.

She stood in front of the mirror on the shop floor, trying to hide her grin of delight as she looked at herself in her new cream jodhpurs, brown jodhpur boots, dark gloves, dark brown tweed jacket, shirt, tie and new velvet riding hat. On the chair beside her was a pair of long black boots for wearing if she was riding the larger ponies. On the way to the saddlers, Len had explained to her that every class had its own specific dress code.

'You'll do,' he commented now.

Ellie smoothed down the jacket with a gloved hand – she was really looking forward to competing. She wished Joe was more into shows, so she could go home and show him her new outfit. Luke would understand, but she was hardly likely to go and show off her clothes to him.

Instead, she told Spirit about the trip when she got back. Each day the bond between them was growing stronger and she spent every second she could just being with him. He was putting on weight now and his injuries were slowly starting to heal.

On Thursday Ellie woke up to the sound of rain beating down on the bedroom window. Forcing herself out of her warm bed, she threw on some clothes. When she went outside, the rain lashed against her, soaking her hair and finding its way down her collar. She splashed through the puddles and went up to the feedroom where her uncle was giving out feeds. It was a miserable day to be up so early, and she and Joe exchanged commiseratory looks as they walked round the courtyard with the feedbuckets.

The rain continued all morning, driving down from the mountain. It was too wet to ride and so the horses and ponies were turned out in the fields. Ellie turned Spirit out with some of the others while she mucked out his stable. She hated it when it rained like this. The grey sky felt so heavy it seemed to press down on the dull green and brown fields, and she felt like she was being squashed. It made her long for the summer in New Zealand where the sun shone on the large, rolling fields and the skies were wide and cornflower-blue.

Sighing, she finished the stable and went down

the field to catch Spirit. The mud was thick around the gate and the short winter grass slippery underfoot. Three of the horses were trotting around near the bottom of the field, one nipping the others, making them buck and throw their heads up. Spirit was staying out of trouble as usual, grazing peacefully. Gem, Wisp and Picasso were beside him. Ellie had noticed that the quieter horses often seemed to gravitate towards him. She called out his name, but in the rain he didn't hear her. Ellie began to squelch through the mud and across the grass. 'Come on, boy!' she called, not wanting to have to walk all the way down the field.

Spirit noticed her and, pricking his ears, he started to head towards her, but as he did so something startled the three horses near the bottom of the field. They leapt forwards. Gem, Wisp and Picasso's heads flew up at the sound of the others and they began to canter. The six horses were caught up in each other's alarm. Ellie stopped, but her feet slipped on the wet ground. She felt herself bang down on her side as her fingers closed on mud. There was a yell from behind her.

The next few minutes seemed to happen in slow motion. Pushing herself up on her arms, Ellie saw the six horses galloping straight for her through the rain, too caught up in each other's fear to notice her lying there. Even if they did see her, it would be too late for them to stop. Ellie cried out and curled up into a ball, bracing herself.

She felt rather than saw Spirit reach her. Before Ellie knew what was happening, her eyes blinked open to see Spirit standing over her, his legs on either side of her body. She felt his strong reassuring presence as the other horses thundered by. They broke into a trot as they finally realized there was nothing to be scared of, and Ellie heard their snorts and the sound of their hooves slowing as they began to circle round, tails high.

Ellie's heart hammered against her ribs. For a moment she was too shaken to move. Her eyes flicked from side to side and then Spirit stepped carefully over her, picking his hooves up high so he didn't touch her at all. He stopped at the side, his head by hers.

Ellie slowly uncurled and sat up. Spirit nudged at her with his muzzle, anxiously touching her knees and her face as if checking she was OK. The rain dripped from his eyelashes and down his face.

'Ellie! Ellie! Are you all right?' She looked round. Joe was running down the field through the rain.

'Yes.' Putting a hand on Spirit's leg, Ellie struggled to her feet. Her own legs felt like jelly. 'Yes, I'm OK.'

Joe reached her, his face pale. 'I was by the gate. I saw what happened. I thought you were going to be trampled!'

'Spirit saved me,' Ellie stammered, as she kept stroking the grey horse over and over again.

'I know,' Joe said in awe. 'He just stood in their path and they went round him. I've never seen anything like it.'

Ellie swallowed. 'Thank you,' she whispered to Spirit.

Together, the three of them walked up the field, Ellie holding shakily on to Spirit's mane.

For the rest of the day, she thought about what her horse had done. He'd seen her fall, stood over her, shielded her and protected her.

'You're amazing,' she told him gratefully when she went to his stable after supper. The rain had now turned to sleet. The fields were waterlogged and it was freezing cold. Closing her eyes, she put her arms round Spirit's neck and hugged him. She was so tired. It had been a very long day. She'd planned to give Spirit a proper groom but now she just couldn't find the energy. Instead, she just stood there, stroking his head and neck, too exhausted to do anything but be with him. He sighed contentedly, his eyes half closing as she ran her hands over his forehead and down his nose and cheeks.

She didn't know how it happened, but very gradually Ellie became aware of a shift in the atmosphere around them. She couldn't describe the feeling exactly, but it was almost as though there was a field of energy surrounding each of them and it was somehow merging. She opened her eyes and saw that Spirit was staring straight at her. As their gaze met, a connection flared and Ellie was aware of images and feelings coming into her mind. She saw the tall figure of a man at a stable door and fear ran through her. The bolts on the door pulled back with a loud metal clang and the man stood in the doorway, whip in hand. She knew she wanted to run, but there was nowhere to go. Leaping forward, she was stopped by the manger. The man shut the door behind him and approached, the whip raised, his eyes angry. She tried to jump past him but heard the whistle as the whip came slashing down; she felt the terror as it hit her neck, a searing biting pain –

No!

Ellie blinked and recoiled. The pictures stopped.

She stared at Spirit, her heart thumping, the feelings of terror fading as she realized she was in the stable with him. What had just happened? Those awful pictures in her head . . .

They'd seemed so vivid, so real. Shakily, she reached out a hand and touched Spirit's face again. It was as though she had seen into his mind – seen his memories, seen why he was now so scared when the door bolts on his stable were pulled back. But that was impossible.

Ellie shook her head. Yet even as the logical part of her mind protested at what had just happened, an instinctive deeper part of her knew it was true – as true as the fact that sleet was falling outside the stable.

She hesitated and then threw herself open again to the feeling.

Spirit? she thought, half-wondering what she was doing.

There was the same shift in energy . . .

The whip slashed down again and again. She wasn't Ellie any more. She became Spirit, feeling what he had felt, seeing what he had seen. As the whip beat into her, she felt his unbearable pain and confusion. *I didn't mean to be bad. I didn't understand. Stop, please, stop!*

The memory suddenly changed.

Cold, wet, hungry. Outside. She could feel the wind blowing down the mountain, feel the ache in her legs as she trudged up an uneven hill in the rain. There was a heavy rider on her back, a beginner, he was unsteady and she could smell stale beer on his breath. His hands grabbed at the cold bit, using the reins to balance his weight. 'Gee up, you lazy devil!'

I'm trying. Please, I'm trying.

Spirit's back – *her* back – was hurting. Her tendons were sore from overwork. She stumbled, one shoe loose. The man slapped her again with the whip.

Get off me. The thought swelled through her mind as the whip fell again, and this time she couldn't bear it any longer; she reared up. The man's weight fell to one side, his hands yanking at the bit. Tired, weak and hungry, she hadn't strength enough left to stay on her feet. She twisted in the air, crashing down on the stony ground, landing with her whole weight on her shoulder – and the man.

Lying there, she heard the chaos, the people from the trekking centre yelling, the man being pulled out from underneath, swearing and clutching his leg. The rain beat down and the people shouted . . .

Ellie opened her eyes. The air in the stable was very still. Neither she nor Spirit was moving. It was as though they were standing together in a spotlight, the rest of the world having faded to black around them.

She stared at him, horror sharp inside. 'All the things that people have done to you.'

Spirit regarded her steadily. Putting her hands on the left side of his neck where she had felt the first whip blows, she stroked down, wishing she could change what had happened and take away the pain. No horse should ever have to feel like that. Not ever. Ellie shuddered at the memories. Now she knew how he had felt, it was almost too much to bear. Undoing his rug, she stroked gently over his whole body, sweeping down over his shoulder where he had fallen, across his back that had been so sore, over his ribs which had been so bruised. Spirit stood absolutely still until she reached his head again and then he snorted. His eyes were softer than she had ever seen them. He nuzzled her and then stepped away, taking a long drink before going to his haynet. Ellie rugged him up, functioning on autopilot, not thinking, just doing. Whatever had just happened was too big for her to get her mind round quickly. She fastened the front buckle of his rug, rested her head against his for a moment, and then kissed him.

'I'll see you in the morning,' she whispered, dazed.

She hurried into the house, thankful not to see anyone as she took off her boots and coat. She ran all the way up to her room, washed in the bathroom and got into her pyjamas. Then she got into bed and lay there, letting herself start to think about it all.

She didn't know how but she was sure she'd seen into Spirit's mind. He had sent her pictures and thoughts. In his own way, he had communicated with her.

She shook her head. *But how? How? How?*

Deep down, though, she knew that right now *how* wasn't important; what mattered was that it had happened. And it had. It really had.

Curling up on her side, Ellie put her arms round her knees. Pictures flooded through her mind, thoughts, questions. She replayed the whole thing. She knew now why the sound of his stable door opening scared

Spirit so much. She knew why his shoulder was scarred. She knew part of where he had come from – where he had been. Would he communicate with her again? She hardly dared to hope.

Don't be stupid, she told herself. *There's no way it will happen again.*

But what if it does?

It was a long, long time before Ellie got to sleep that night.

Chapter Nine

The harsh sound of the alarm pulled Ellie from a deep sleep. Eyes still shut, she reached for the clock, but then suddenly everything from the night before flashed into her mind and her eyes shot open. *Spirit!*

Remembering what had happened, she threw back the covers, furious with herself for not waking earlier. If she'd got up sooner, she could have gone down to his stable and seen if the same thing could happen again. But it was too late now. In fifteen minutes everyone would be out on the yard.

Pulling on some clothes, she hurried outside, desperate for a few moments alone with Spirit. It was bitterly cold still, but the rain and sleet had stopped. The horses were looking over their doors, banging their hooves impatiently against the wood as she ran past. The cats came trotting past the puddles, tails high, mewing at the thought of breakfast, but Ellie ignored them all.

When she reached Spirit's stable, she was taken

aback by how ordinary he looked. He had straw in his white tail and his stable rug was hanging slightly to one side. But what had she been expecting? That'd he'd have sparkles floating round him or something?

However, as their eyes met, Ellie saw an understanding there and suddenly she knew with an absolute, unshakable certainty that the evening before had happened just as she remembered it. She touched Spirit wonderingly. She couldn't quite get her head round it, but suddenly her life felt totally different, almost as if she had discovered a completely new colour. She and Spirit had somehow connected. What now? It was as if she was standing on the edge of a cliff, looking down from a great height, not knowing what was beneath her or what would happen if she jumped.

'What happens next?' Ellie asked him helplessly.

Outside, she heard the sound of stable doors opening on the yard and people calling to each other. She couldn't stay long with Spirit now or she'd be in trouble.

'I'll see you later,' she whispered to him. Trying to compose herself and look normal, she headed to the feedroom.

Ellie might have tried to look normal but her thoughts were all over the place. She got shouted at for mixing up Gabriel and Hereward's feeds and then for tripping up with a wheelbarrow and spilling dirty straw all over the yard. When she started riding, Picasso sensed her distraction and played up, snatching at the bit and repeatedly shying away from one corner of the school.

Len watched in the centre, his face growing darker by the second. 'You're riding like a sack of ruddy potatoes. Get him together! Come on!' His voice rose. 'Make him go into that corner! NOW!'

Ellie used her legs hard. Picasso's ears flattened, but he decided not to argue any more. However, a little while later when she started thinking about Spirit again he decided to throw in a buck and she almost flew over his head. Taking advantage of the fact that she had lost her reins and balance, he shot off down the school, swerving round Luke on Starlight.

Len exploded with a string of swear words as, red in the face, Ellie grabbed her reins back and sat up.

'For Christ's sake, Ellie!' Len thundered. 'Get your act together! You've got your first flamin' show to go to in three weeks.'

'If we can get him into the lorry,' muttered Joe, who was schooling Wisp at the end of the school. Picasso had refused to go into a horsebox since his aborted visit to the show.

Joe gave Ellie a look of sympathy as she turned Picasso round, but Luke just grinned at her as she rode back up the school, her heart in her boots.

'You're going to have to ride better than that,' he said.

Face still red, Ellie kept her attention on Picasso and rode him into place again behind Starlight.

Len continued to shout at her all lesson and she was very glad when it was time to take Picasso in.

At lunchtime Ellie breathed a massive sigh of relief as everyone else headed off the yard and she had a chance to be with Spirit on her own. Her fingers shook as she took off his rug. What was going to happen? Would it be like the night before? Would she be able to communicate with him and see his memories?

She was so excited she found it hard to stand still. She tried touching his neck, but although he nuzzled her shoulders nothing happened. She moved impatiently to his head and stroked his face, waiting for some pictures to come into her mind. But none did. She ran her hands over him. *Come on, come on*, she thought. *Talk to me, Spirit*. But there was nothing. Eventually Ellie stood back, disappointment lying over her. It wasn't happening.

She tried to remember what she'd been doing when it had started the evening before. *I was just standing with him*, she realized, *standing still*.

Spirit was pulling at his hay now. Ellie faced him, one hand either side of his neck as he pulled and chewed. Shutting her eyes, she breathed slowly in and out, until the impatience drained away and she was left with a feeling of calm. The space inside her where the energy had been buzzing filled with thoughts of Spirit.

Breathe in. Breathe out.

She thought about wanting to help him. Thought about wanting to take away his pain.

Breathe in. Breathe out.

Standing there, Ellie became vaguely aware that Spirit had stopped eating and was now standing still too. She could feel him breathing, her hands still resting on his neck. A warm glow seemed to wrap around them both.

I'm here, she told him, the words coming from deep inside her without her even thinking about them. *I'm listening.*

A connection surged between them again. Memories came into her mind. Like the night before, they weren't hers, but she could see them as clearly as if they were. She saw the same mountainside and felt the weight of the man on her back again. She felt the rain driving down and the rough stony ground under her hooves.

Was this where you were before you came here? she asked him.

Yes.

Ellie started, her eyes opening involuntarily. She

stared at Spirit. She had asked him a question and he had answered her!

Pushing away her wonder, she shut her eyes and let her mind go blank again. The pictures filled it straight away. She saw a tumbledown row of stables, a steaming untidy muck heap sprawling over cobbles, a stony yard littered with weeds, loose straw and bale string. The yard was in a valley, with tracks leading up steep mountains. Horses hung their heads over the doors, not with pricked ears and eager expressions like the horses on her uncle's yard – these horses looked empty-eyed and defeated. An aura of sadness and pain surrounded them all.

In her mind, Ellie interpreted what she was seeing, turning the pictures into human words. *It was a trekking centre in the mountains. You weren't treated well,* she thought to Spirit. *You weren't fed much, were you? You and the other horses were in pain and tired?*

Waves of energy rolled off Spirit as he answered her. *Yes. Yes.*

More pictures shifted through Ellie's brain as he showed her what it had been like. People coming to ride. Beginners who sat heavily in the saddle. The riding stable owner and a groom who worked for her, shouting at the horses. Never checking them for injuries or aches. Never offering them kindness. The only soft word coming from the occasional trekker who stroked them and offered love.

I tried so hard. Ellie could feel deep in her heart what Spirit was saying. *I wanted to be good.*

She could feel his hunger, feel his pain, feel the ill-fitting saddle pressing into his spine and the rub of the rough, grass-encrusted bit in his sensitive mouth. She could hear the shouts in his ears, while all the time he had just wanted to please. It was almost too much to bear.

Instinctively she hugged him. Spirit pushed his nose against her back. She stood for a long moment, drawing up all the strength she had and trying to give it to him.

After a few minutes he breathed out deeply, a sigh of release and relief.

He stepped back and she felt the connection weaken. She knew he'd had enough for the moment.

Ellie leant against the stable wall. Again she had the same feeling she'd had that morning, the feeling of life having somehow shifted. It was as though she was now looking at it from a different angle. She had no words to explain quite what was happening between them but she knew that her life would never be the same again.

She was no longer standing on the edge of the precipice; she had well and truly jumped off.

Chapter Ten

'Joe! Joe!'

Joe had been collecting empty haynets. Ellie raced up to him. 'I've got to talk to you!'

'Why?'

Ellie hesitated. How did she start? *I can talk to Spirit* . . . . Joe would think she'd gone mad. *Spirit's telling me stuff* . . . That was just as bad.

'Well?' Joe pressed.

'Um, it's Spirit.'

'He's OK, isn't he?' Joe's brow furrowed.

'Yeah – yeah, he's fine. It's just . . .' Ellie chose her words carefully. 'Look, promise you won't think I'm mad, but I think I can communicate with him. Really communicate.' She could feel her eyes sparkling despite her worries about telling him. 'It's like I can talk to him. He's telling me things about his life and . . .' Joe's eyebrows had risen. 'It's true!'

'Yeah, right. Hey, look, was that something pink with a curly tail I saw flapping past?' Joe grinned.

'Joe!' Ellie exclaimed, stamping her foot in frustration. 'I mean it!'

'That you can talk to Spirit?' Joe looked disbelieving.

'Well, not talk exactly.' Ellie struggled to explain. 'Not like chat in words. It's mainly pictures and feeling stuff.'

'So, what's he been telling you?' Joe said, but from his tone Ellie could tell that he still didn't believe her.

'Oh, forget it. It doesn't matter.' Disappointment flooded through her. She'd really wanted to share it with Joe. She'd hoped he'd get it. But maybe it was too much to expect. It was pretty bizarre. 'I'm just being stupid.' She forced a smile. 'Joke!' She saw Joe's relieved smile in return. 'So, what do we have to do this afternoon? Did your dad say?' she asked, quickly changing the subject.

'Yeah, tidy the muck heap.'

Ellie sighed. 'Great.' It was her least favourite task.

After she and Joe had swept up all the loose straw, flattened the top of the muck heap and made it into the perfectly rectangular shape that Len liked, she went back to Spirit's stable, still feeling a bit let down that Joe hadn't believed her. She stood looking at the door for a few minutes, and then fetched some bale string and a screwdriver and a metal hook from the toolbox in the tackroom.

Fifteen minutes later, she stood back, satisfied. She had removed the bolts and the door was now fastened with a plaited rope of bale string that ran through two hooks. She tied it in a quick-release knot. She could undo it and open the door without a sound.

'Hi, Ellie,' Stuart said, walking over. He nodded at the stable door. 'What are you doing?'

'I think the noise of the bolt was scaring Spirit whenever it was opened,' Ellie explained. 'That maybe something happened in his past and the noise of the bolt reminded him of it. He might relax more without it.'

Ellie hoped Stuart wouldn't be cross. To her relief, he nodded in approval. 'Good idea. Look, when you've finished can you come and help me with Milly for a while? I need to pull her mane.'

'Sure. I'm done here.' Ellie followed Stuart up to the clipping barn where Milly was tied up. The little chestnut didn't like having her flaxen mane pulled to shorten and thin it, and had to have one of her front legs held up otherwise she would move around too much.

Stuart got out the mane comb and Ellie picked up Milly's left front hoof. As Stuart worked, pushing the comb down the mane and pulling a few strands out at a time, Ellie studied his face. The more she got to know him the more she liked him; he was quiet but kind and he knew so much about horses.

'How did you come to work here, Stuart?' she asked curiously.

'I met your uncle when I was working at a racing stables. We got on and he asked me if I'd come and work for him. Racing's a young man's game and so I said yes as soon as he asked. He taught me all about the showing world – he knows his horses and he treats them well. He may seem harsh and he hasn't time for hangers-on, but the horses who are here, well, they have a good life. They go out in the field, work, get top-rate food and lots of grooming. If I was a horse I'd want to be here.'

'Unless you were old or lame,' muttered Ellie. Joe had told her stories about horses and ponies that her uncle had got rid of when they were unable to show any more.

Stuart chuckled. 'Well, there is that. Your uncle's no time for sentiment, but that doesn't make him a bad man. And he's helped a fair few problem horses in his time. Horses other people would have shown the bullet to.'

Ellie didn't say anything and Stuart worked on in silence, whistling through his teeth as he thinned Milly's mane.

Ellie wondered what *he* would say if he knew about Spirit talking to her. 'Stuart,' she said hesitantly. 'Have you ever heard about people talking to horses, properly talking?'

Stuart frowned. 'You mean like when someone's a horse whisperer?'

Ellie shook her head. She knew horse whisperers were people who worked with problem horses by building up a relationship with the horse and trying to figure out what was going on in the horse's head. She'd never heard of them actually talking to a horse the way she had with Spirit. 'No, I mean have you ever heard of anyone who can really talk to a horse, ask it questions and stuff?'

She waited for Stuart to laugh, but he looked thoughtful.

'There was a lady I met when I was at the racing yard. She reckoned she could talk to horses. She was a friend of the trainer's.'

Ellie was astonished. 'What?'

'Yeah. Nice lady. Quite normal-looking, you know. Like someone's mum. She used to come down to the yard and then stand there, listening to the horses who weren't behaving right. She'd ask them questions in her head and afterwards she'd tell you what was wrong with them.' Stuart shook his own head. 'I don't know. It was probably just a fluke, but a lot of the time she did seem to work out what was the matter with them. She used to say that everyone could talk to horses if they tried but that some people were better at it than others; it was a case of . . .' He frowned for a moment, trying to remember. 'Tuning into the horses' energy or something. She'd been doing it all her life.' He grinned at Ellie. 'Why the interest? You thinking of getting someone like that for Spirit? That'd finish the boss off, that would. He doesn't hold with any of that stuff, you know.'

Ellie smiled quickly. 'It's OK. I'm not thinking about it.' She looked down quickly at Milly's hoof. Her thoughts were buzzing. Perhaps people *could* talk to horses then. If the lady that Stuart had met was to be believed lots of people could, although it seemed some people could do it more easily than others. *Maybe I'm one of those people*, thought Ellie. She wondered if she could talk to horses other than Spirit.

Stuart chuckled and nodded at Milly who was looking very fed up. 'Glad I can't hear her talk. Right now, she would be saying, "Get off my bloody mane!" and a whole load more besides.' He patted the pony. 'All done now, though, girl.'

Ellie put Milly away and then went to groom Picasso. There was no one else in the ponies' barn. It was the perfect opportunity to try and talk to him. Ellie tied him up and, remembering what she had done with Spirit, tried to stand still and make her mind go blank. *Talk to me*, she thought eagerly to the pony. *I'm listening.*

Nothing happened. Picasso watched her with his usual aloofness. She tried stroking him, talking to him in her head.

She waited some more, but the change in the atmosphere never came. She never felt that strange sensation of their minds merging and becoming one.

Disappointment surged through her. Maybe it didn't work with other horses. But she comforted herself with the thought that at least she could talk to Spirit, and maybe one day she would learn how to talk to others too. *Perhaps I just have to get better at it*, she thought hopefully.

Picking up the body brush and curry comb, she began to groom.

That evening she went to Spirit's stable. He was pulling at his haynet and his eyes looked calmer. It was as though the very fact that he had been able to share his thoughts and fears had already helped him in some way.

'And your legs are definitely looking better too,' Ellie murmured happily, glancing at his tendons. Going into the stable, she ran a hand down them. The poulticing had done them good and they felt harder and cooler to the touch. Spirit nuzzled her back as she knelt beside him. Smiling, she rubbed his neck. Then she waited, emptying her mind.

Gradually she felt Spirit's thoughts come to her. He showed her a picture of his stable door with the bale string she had fixed and she felt an intense feeling of relief. *Thank you.*

That's OK. I just want to help, she told him.

A thrill ran through her as she realized she was talking to him again, really talking. She thought back to the memories they had shared that morning. *Where were you before you want to the trekking centre?*

A picture of the tall man with the whip came into her mind.

Who was he?

Ellie saw Spirit travelling in a horsebox. The journey ended with a jolt and there was a rush of light as the ramp banged down. A groom led him out on to a smart yard. She could sense the nervous energy about the Arab horses looking over the white stable doors. They paced around, tossing their heads.

Pictures flashed through her mind like a slide show. The horses being led out in hand and ridden, taken to shows, but never going out in the fields, never being allowed to roll and play. They had good food – lots of it. It fattened them up, but also gave them so much energy that when they did go out of their stables they pranced and fought for their heads. The tall man was in charge. He was a good rider but hard, demanding instant obedience. The bit in Spirit's mouth was harsh and the man wore spurs. Ellie felt Spirit's confusion, torn between the energy that was rushing through him and the man exerting absolute control.

The picture changed and she saw Spirit one night, lying down in the stable, stuck against the wall. He kicked and struggled before finally freeing himself with a twist and getting to his feet, but she could sense the pain in his back now. When the man came the next day, no one could see the pain but it was there. As the saddle was put on, the pain increased. Spirit kicked out but the groom just shouted and hit him in the stomach.

It hurt.

The tall man took him to the school and tried to mount.

No. Spirit sidled round and was smacked again. The man swung himself into the saddle and Ellie gasped as a red-hot needle of pain shot through her own back. She saw Spirit squeal and buck, throwing the man off on to the ground. The man got to his feet, shouting. He walked over, Spirit tried to shoot away.

I tried to tell him. I tried to stop him.

The man called two more grooms to help. They forced Spirit still while the man mounted again, but the second his weight hit the saddle the pain jabbed again. Half-maddened, Spirit reared up and then plunged forward, bucking like a wild thing until the man hit the ground. This time he didn't get up so quickly.

Spirit was led back to the stall. Ellie felt his relief at having the saddle taken off and then his fear as a tall figure loomed in the doorway. The bolts slid back and the man came in, whip in hand.

I'd tried to stop him riding me. I tried to tell him about the pain. I didn't mean to be bad . . .

She saw the whip raised, heard it slashing down through the air and felt it bite into her, and then the pictures stopped.

Ellie took a deep trembling breath. She knew the physical pain from the beating had left Spirit, but the fear and confusion still filled his mind.

He looked at her. *Why?*

Ellie swallowed, not knowing what to say. What answer could she give? Because people can and do? She hated it but it was true. Sometimes bad stuff happened because people were ignorant or cruel. *And sometimes it just happens because life's like that*, she thought, feeling desolate as an image of her mum and dad filled her mind. She had a flashback to the day before they'd died in the crash. They'd been getting ready to go away, arguing in a good-humoured way as they packed.

Ellie's eyes stung with tears. She started to force the memory away, but just then Spirit turned his head and nuzzled her shoulder. She could feel the softness of his skin, feel the love coming from him, and sensed him asking her about it. Swallowing, she let herself remember.

'Come on, Ellie. Your mum doesn't need all these

things. Tell her.' She could hear her dad's voice. 'You're on my side, aren't you?' he'd appealed.

'Nope!' She'd darted over to the bed and picked up the pile of books and clothes her dad had just taken out of her mum's packed suitcase. 'You can never take too many books and clothes.' She'd dumped them back in the suitcase and her dad had tickled her.

She'd squealed and tripped over, almost falling on top of her mum who'd grabbed a hairbrush and brandished it at Ellie's dad. 'You will not take my clothes and books!'

'Honestly! You girls!' Rolling his eyes at them both, her dad had left the room.

Her mum had laughed and put her arms round Ellie. Ellie remembered the faint scent of her, felt the softness of her cheek against hers.

'I'm going to miss you, sweetie. Are you sure you'll be OK without us?'

Ellie knew she had grinned. 'Course I will.'

Now her throat constricted. *I didn't mean forever, Mum*. Grief overwhelmed her. *Why did it have to happen? Why? Oh, Mum. Dad. I want you back.*

Wrapping her arms round Spirit's neck, Ellie sobbed. Not the hopeless tears she used to cry in the nights when she had first arrived at the farm – not the tears that had seeped silently down her cheeks like water overflowing from a too-full cup, but great wracking sobs that came from deep down inside her, shaking her shoulders, contorting her face, making her gasp for breath.

Eventually she became aware of Spirit breathing quietly on her back. Her sobs quietened until she was simply resting against him, her tears drying on her face. She felt exhausted, drained, like her mind had somehow been emptied.

Spirit's neck was solid under her fingers and she leant against him, drawing comfort. Her parents and her old life might have gone, but Spirit was real, warm and alive, and neither of them were alone any more now they had each other.

Chapter Eleven

Over the next few weeks, Ellie was kept very busy on the yard. Joe had his exams coming up and was revising hard, and her uncle was intent on getting her ready to go in the first big spring show on Picasso. 'It'll be good to get a win under your belt early on in the season.'

If I win, Ellie thought. But her uncle wasn't the sort of person who dealt in *ifs*. She did all she could, schooling Picasso and hacking him out, grooming him until he shone. And she wasn't just busy with Picasso; there were the other ponies to ride too, and the larger horses were all back in proper work now with their show season fast approaching. Ellie helped with exercising them. But no matter how tired she was, or how hard she had been working, she went to Spirit's stable every night after supper to speak to him.

Sometimes she learnt more about his life and past and other times she would talk to him, telling him about her mum and dad, showing him the pictures in her head – the times she'd been out with her dad on his vet rounds, riding with her mum, bedtime stories, even the times when she'd got into trouble and been told off or the times she'd argued with them. And when the memories made her cry Spirit would stand still, breathing gently on her skin.

Equally, Ellie listened as he told her about his life. She worked out that he must have been at the trek-king centre for four years because he showed her four cold winters passing. After he had fallen on his shoulder and been too lame to ride, he had been put out in a muddy field until he had been taken to the sale, lame, half-starved and neglected. Ellie felt his suffering as he showed her his past and she gave him all the love she could.

Was your life always bad? she asked him one day.
No.

He showed her times when he had been at a large riding school and treated fairly, but then a blurry picture of a green field filled her mind. There was a white-grey mare and a middle-aged woman in it. A glow seemed to surround them, and as she looked at the picture Ellie felt deep love and deep loss. These were long-ago memories of soft hands, soft voices, laughter. Joyful at the time, but edged with sadness because they were gone.

They were happy times for you, she thought to him. *The best?*

Not the best.

A picture of herself suddenly appeared in her mind. She saw herself as Spirit saw her, blonde hair coming out from under a woollen hat, jodhpurs covered with hayseeds, gloves dirty. She felt a deep sense of love and happiness coming from him.

'You mean now is the best?' she whispered.

Spirit breathed on her hands. *Yes*.

Whenever she had the time, Ellie led Spirit out down the lane, gently exercising him to build his muscles up. As February changed to March, Spirit's lameness disappeared and he started to put on weight. He was devoted to Ellie but still wary of most other people, although he would tolerate Stuart leading him out or rugging him up if Ellie was at school. He was a different horse in the field, though – relaxed and confident. Whenever he was grazing, there would usually be at least three or four other horses around him, and wherever he moved they would follow. *His fan club*, Joe joked.

'Spirit's a good horse,' Stuart told Ellie as they groomed Picasso before the big show in mid-March. 'The others trust him. He's like Merlin in that I know I can put him out with anyone. Horses like that are worth their weight in gold on a yard.'

Ellie glowed. It was rare anyone said anything nice about Spirit. She knew Sasha and Helen didn't like

Spirit because he put his ears back and threatened with his teeth if they went in the stable with him. Luke just laughed at him and called him 'the old nag'. Len ignored him.

'You've done a good job with him,' Stuart went on. 'He's not an easy horse, but you've made a real difference so far. Have you tried riding him yet?'

Ellie shook her head. She was longing to but she didn't want to rush things.

'You should.' Stuart patted Picasso. 'Right, that's you ready, lad.'

'Do you think he'll go into the horsebox?' Ellie asked.

The bay pony was still completely refusing to load.

'If he doesn't, there'll be no show tomorrow. Joe and I are planning to have another try at getting him in at lunchtime today. If we take our time, hopefully we'll manage it.'

Ellie went to put the grooming kit away in the tackroom. Luke was in one corner with Sasha. He had his arms on the wall on either side of her and she was smiling up at him. Their faces were very close together, and Ellie had the feeling that if she had come in a moment sooner she would have caught them kissing.

She expected them to spring apart guiltily but they didn't. Luke gave her a lazy grin.

'Well, don't mind me!' she muttered, marching across the tackroom to put the bridle away.

'Thanks,' Luke said, turning back to Sasha. 'We won't.'

Ellie felt a rush of irritation. They could at least have the decency to look embarrassed.

'I should go,' she heard Sasha say.

'Stay,' Luke said, his voice holding a smile.

Sasha giggled and pulled away. 'I can't!' She ducked out under his arm. 'See you later,' she said, and then she vanished out of the tackroom door.

Ellie looked at Luke in disbelief. 'I thought you had a girlfriend already.'

'Yes,' he agreed.

'And that's not a problem for you?'

'Jealous?' he said, raising his eyebrows.

A cross exclamation burst from her. 'In your dreams!'

'Don't you mean my nightmares, Ellie!' Luke grinned at her outraged expression. 'So, how's that old nag of yours doing?' he went on, turning to pick up a bridle.

'He's not an old nag!'

'OK, so how's –' Luke made his voice sound deep and dramatic – '*Spirit*.'

Ellie glared at him. 'Fine.'

'You'll never make your money back when you sell him.'

'I don't want to make my money back! I'm not going to sell him.'

Luke raised his eyebrows. 'Have you told that to Len? He's not going to budge on that one, you know. If I were you, I'd get used to the thought of that horse of yours leaving. After all, it's almost six weeks since you bought him, isn't it?'

Luke's words sent a prickle of foreboding through Ellie. Her uncle hadn't said anything recently about Spirit going, but that didn't mean he had forgotten the deal they'd made.

He won't really make me sell Spirit, she thought anxiously. *Will he?*

Ellie tried not to think about it. At lunchtime she put Spirit's bridle on and took him for a walk down the drive. As she led him through the courtyard, several of the other horses whinnied to him. Ellie smiled, remembering what Stuart had said earlier. 'They all like you, boy.'

When she reached the car park, she saw Stuart and Joe trying to load Picasso. They were looking hot and the bay pony's coat was streaked with sweat. He was refusing to go anywhere near the horsebox. Ellie could feel the waves of fear coming off him every time he looked at the lorry.

Since she had started communicating with Spirit she'd found that even though she might not be able to talk to other horses in the same way she could to Spirit, she could often feel their emotions very clearly – even more than she had before.

'Come on, Picasso,' Joe said, sighing and sitting on the ramp. 'Look, there's nothing to be frightened of.'

But Picasso rolled his eyes and tried to cart Stuart away. He whinnied as he caught sight of Spirit and pulled towards him. Stuart let him come over.

'No luck then?' Ellie said.

'No.' Stuart shook his head. 'I don't know what we're going to do. He's got himself into such a state he's never going to go in. The boss will go mad. I reckon we just have to give him a break now and then try again later. If all else fails we'll have to scrap the show tomorrow and spend the next few weeks working on it. We could sedate him and get him in, then hopefully make him see there's nothing to be frightened of – feed him in there, take him for short journeys. But we can't sedate him for a show, he wouldn't be able to compete.'

Ellie felt a stab of disappointment as she stroked Picasso's damp neck. She'd been really looking forward to the next day. *Please go in, please*, she silently urged the pony. It wasn't just the show, though. After all, she knew there would be many other shows to go to in the future. It was just that sedating him and forcing him in there while he couldn't resist felt so wrong.

'Let's try once more,' Stuart said, patting his neck.

'Good luck with it.' Saying goodbye to Stuart and Joe, Ellie led Spirit away up the lane.

Spirit walked out eagerly, his ears pricked, eyes inquisitive. His mane and forelock were long and silky now, and although his legs were still scarred he was slowly starting to build up muscle. He looked so much better.

She let him pause to rub his face on a fence post. On either side of the lane there were fields of sheep with small lambs, and the sun was fighting through the white clouds. There wasn't much warmth in its rays, but it was very welcome after the bleak January and February. Looking around, Ellie could see daffodils pushing upwards and the green buds on the trees. She had a feeling of the landscape thawing, life breaking out on the barren slopes.

Putting her arm over Spirit's withers, she felt content – happy to be where she was. She remembered what Stuart had said about riding Spirit. If she stepped up on the first plank of the fence she would be able to get on . . .

But should she?

Deep down, she knew she should wait until she was back at the yard with a saddle and people around in the safety of the school. It was madness to try and get on Spirit's back now, but it also felt right, and she was learning to trust her instincts.

Standing up on the fence, Ellie leant her weight over Spirit's back. His ears twitched, but he didn't move.

'Can I get on you?' she asked, feeling somehow that it was right to ask his permission.

He stayed still. She hesitated. She was sure he was OK with it. Putting her trust in him, she moved her right leg over his hindquarters and slowly sat up. Spirit tensed.

'It's OK,' she murmured, trying to stay relaxed. She knew if she tensed up too, then he would think there was something to be afraid of. She breathed out, letting her energy flow down through him. His back felt warm underneath her. 'There, Spirit. Good boy.' Her fingers stroked his neck and mane.

She continued murmuring to him until she felt him lower his head and relax. Should she get off, make that do?

Spirit made the decision for her. Turning from the fence, he started to walk down the lane. Ellie quickly gathered up the reins, but kept her hands as light as possible. She could remember the way his mouth had been hurt in the past. She let her legs hang down loosely. She'd ridden Abbey many times bareback, usually when she was feeling too lazy to tack her up properly. Spirit had a long, smooth stride. He walked out, his ears pricked, and she had the feeling he was happy to be ridden.

At the end of the driveway there was a road, and on the far side of the road a small wood with a bridlepath through it. Spirit pulled eagerly at the bit and Ellie let him cross. As his hooves fell on the soft grass and soil of the woods, he broke into a jog.

Ellie released his head slightly and the next moment he had plunged forward. 'Steady, boy,' she gasped, tightening her hold on the reins as the speed took her by surprise. He slowed down to a steadier pace. Ellie had to hold on to his mane to stop herself being swept backwards. Exhilaration rushed through her. She was cantering Spirit! He felt amazing – smooth and in control. A bird flew up and he shied, but Ellie moved with him and they cantered on.

At last she drew him back to a trot and then a walk. Eyes shining, she threw her arms round his neck and hugged him tightly before they continued on.

Ellie was still bubbling with happiness as they headed for home. This was just the start. She'd find a saddle that fitted him and then she'd be able to start riding him properly. She couldn't wait to tell Joe. They'd be able to go for rides together. Maybe even jump. 'You're such a good boy,' she said, patting Spirit's neck. 'And I love you so much!'

Just as they got near to the yard, she heard an engine. Her uncle was driving away from the yard towards her. Her heart sank. He was bound to tell her off for riding bareback on the lane. It was too late for her to get off now. She knew she just had to brazen it out. As he drove up, he slowed the car down and lowered the window.

Ellie waited for him to snap but to her surprise he didn't, although his face looked tense.

'So, you're up on him then?' he said.

She nodded warily.

'Good. He's looking better too. You might get an OK price for him now. The next sale's Thursday. We'll get him there for that.'

Ellie felt sick. 'No . . .'

'That was the deal,' Len said curtly. 'We said six weeks, you've had five. Next week he's at the sale and off this yard. You've done well, though. If you want to buy another and bring it on, then I won't stop you.'

The compliment went completely over Ellie's head. All she could think about was the fact that her uncle was going to make her sell Spirit. She'd been pushing the thought to the back of her mind, assuming it wouldn't happen. Five days? That was no time at all!

Her uncle drove on. Heart thudding, Ellie slipped off Spirit's back. Sensing her tension he pushed against her questioningly. She stroked him, her thoughts swirling round.

I'll refuse to sell him.

We did have a deal.

So? I'll break the deal.

As if he'd let you.

Ellie turned to Spirit and he nuzzled her anxiously. 'I'm not letting you go,' she whispered fiercely. 'I'm not!'

Chapter Twelve

Ellie led Spirit back on to the yard. Her legs felt shaky and her thoughts were racing. What was she going to do?

Joe came round the corner from putting Picasso away and saw her face. 'You OK?'

'Yes.' Ellie bit her lip. 'No . . . no, actually, I'm not.' The words tumbled out of her. 'Can we talk?'

'Yeah, sure,' Joe said in surprise. 'Do you want to go to the barn?'

Ellie nodded unhappily. 'I'll just put Spirit away.'

Five minutes later, she ran into the hay barn. Joe was sitting on one of the bales that were sticking out at the bottom of the pile. 'What's wrong?' he asked as Ellie joined him.

Ellie felt her eyes well with tears. 'It's Spirit.' She quickly told him what his dad had said. 'What am I going to do, Joe? I can't sell him.'

Joe looked worried. 'I know you don't want to, but Dad is going to make you stick to the deal.'

'There's got to be some way round it.' Ellie remembered what she had first thought when she'd bought Spirit. 'Maybe I could keep him somewhere else?'

'But there isn't another stables for several miles. How would you get there?'

Ellie searched for an answer. 'Cycle?'

Joe shook his head. 'It's just not possible. You couldn't cycle there and back in the dark. It would be much too dangerous on those little lanes. Dad would never let you.'

'I'd like to see him try and stop me!'

'Ellie, fighting him isn't going to work,' Joe said quickly. 'You're going to have to just accept this.'

'No way! Come on, Joe,' Ellie appealed desperately. 'You can help me think of something. I can't sell Spirit!' A sob burst from her. She turned quickly away, shutting her eyes tight to stop the tears.

'Oh, Ellie.' She felt Joe's arm round her shoulder. He pulled her against him.

A wave of emotion overwhelmed her. She sobbed into Joe's chest, feeling the comforting strength of his arms. 'I can't bear it! I can't!'

He stroked her hair. 'It'll be OK, Els. Don't cry. We'll think of something.'

Gradually Ellie's tears slowed down. She rubbed Joe's fleece where it was damp from her crying. 'I'm sorry.'

'Don't be daft,' he said softly.

Glancing up at the sound of his reassuring tone, she was caught by the intensity of his gaze. As his eyes searched hers, she suddenly felt as if she was seeing his greeny-grey eyes, his tousled hair and his slightly crooked nose, all for the first time. Joe hastily pulled away, clearing his throat.

'OK. We'll try and work out a plan. A deal, like I said. An offer Dad can't refuse.' His words sounded deceptively normal. But Ellie knew him well enough to hear that there was an unusual tightness in his voice.

She felt confused. This was just Joe in front of her, her best friend, but for one moment it had seemed something more and, from the way he was sounding, she was sure he'd felt it too . . .

'We'd better get back on the yard or people will start looking for us.' Joe went to the barn door and looked back at her. 'You coming?'

As Ellie nodded and stood up, their eyes met for a second. Both of them quickly looked away.

'Hey, I rode Spirit today,' she said wanting to break the suddenly tense silence.

'Really? What happened?' Joe asked. They left the barn and, with Ellie aware that they were both talking just slightly too fast, they walked together down the hill to the yard.

Ellie threw herself into her work that afternoon, trying not to think about the strange moment in the barn. There was enough else to occupy her mind. First of all there was Spirit, and what she was going to do about him. She couldn't sell him. She wouldn't. Particularly not now, after she'd just ridden him for the first time. But what could she do? Her uncle had clearly made his mind up. Five days was no time at all to come up with a plan.

And it wasn't just Spirit she had to worry about, it was Picasso too. Although Joe, Stuart and Len tried again that afternoon, they simply couldn't get the bay pony into the horsebox.

Uttering a string of swear words, Len finally stomped away, having made the decision that they would give up on the idea of taking Picasso to the show next day.

Ellie was disappointed about not going to the show, she couldn't deny it, but her worries about Spirit overshadowed the disappointment. She had to think of a plan. As if to emphasize that he meant what he had said, her uncle left a local newspaper out in the tackroom with an advert for the next horse sale circled with thick red pen.

Ellie thought about it over and over again as she helped to prepare Barney with Darcey and Alfie, two of the clients' horses, for the show. Their legs and tails needed washing and then they all had to be groomed and strapped until their coats were as soft as velvet. The tack had to be cleaned until it was spotless – the leather soft and supple, the bits and stirrups shining like new silver. Then the horsebox had to be loaded up with everything that would be needed – saddles, bridles, grooming kits. And as well as the horses who were going to the show, the other horses needed grooming and looking after too.

'You should be going and I should be riding you,' Ellie told Picasso as she strapped him later that afternoon – banging a leather pad on his neck and hindquarters over and over again to build up his muscles. He was in fantastic condition, his bay coat shining like a piece of dark chocolate, his muscles rippling under his soft skin. 'It's no wonder Uncle Len's mad about you not loading,' she said, sighing. 'You look amazing.'

She wondered if the plan to sedate him to get him used to the horsebox would work. She hoped it would. Joe had told her Picasso loved shows. But if he wouldn't box he couldn't go to any, and if he didn't go to any shows Len would sell him without a doubt.

'Why have you got such a problem with it? What are you scared of?' But, unlike Spirit, Picasso ignored her as he usually did, staring into the distance and fidgeting slightly at the end of his leadrope.

By the time everything was finished, it was after six o'clock. Ellie ate a quick supper of pizza with Joe,

Luke and Len. None of them said much as they sat round the kitchen table. Luke spent most of the meal texting and raising his eyebrows as he read the texts he got back. Joe was quiet. All Len could talk about was the show the next day. And Ellie's thoughts were full of Spirit. Every time she looked at her uncle she wondered how she could persuade him to let Spirit stay.

As soon as they had eaten, Joe hurried away to do some revision, Luke went out and Len sat down to watch the TV. It was Ellie's turn to clear away. She put the plates into the dishwasher and turned it on, crammed the cardboard packets in the recycling bin and then went out to be with Spirit again.

Spirit recognized her footsteps as she came down the yard and, hearing his whinny, Ellie felt her heart lighten. Putting her arms either side of his warm neck, she rested her face against his mane. He swung his head round and rested his muzzle on her right shoulder. She felt as though he was pulling her in tight, hugging her.

'Oh, Spirit. It's been such a busy day. Picasso's not going to the show now because he won't go in the horsebox, and then there's you. I've got to find a way to persuade Uncle Len to let me keep you but I don't know what I can do.' She could feel the panic starting to curl around inside her, building and swirling like smoke from a smouldering bonfire.

Time was ticking away. Thursday loomed large in her mind.

Spirit breathed softly on her hair. Ellie shut her eyes, drawing strength from him. She'd think of something. Her racing thoughts gradually slowed and her mind emptied. A picture came into her mind. But there was something different about it. She frowned, trying to work out why. It was as if the energy wasn't quite the same, she realized. She let herself sink into the picture, wondering what Spirit was showing her.

It was dark. There was a lorry full of foals. There were no partitions and the foals were crammed together, stumbling against each other as the lorry threw them about, hooves grazing each other's delicate legs. The atmosphere was charged with fear and loss. *Mother, mother, mother . . .*

The air was filled with the foals' silent cries, and suddenly she knew the foals were all being taken away from their mothers for the first time. They were very young and terrified. But she had shared Spirit's memories of his first journey away from his mother before and it hadn't been like this. What was going on? Other pictures took over. The lorry stopping. Being herded out into a yard they had never seen before with lots of other ponies there. Shouting. Rough handling. Utter confusion and, running through it all, a deep sense of loss and longing . . .

Picasso came into Ellie's mind. She stared at Spirit. *This isn't you*, she thought. *It's Picasso. Are you showing me what you know about him?*

She felt his answer. *Yes*.

Ellie pieced together Picasso's story from the images Spirit was sending her. The bay pony must have been taken away from his mother when he was very young. He'd had a terrifying journey to a different yard and then he'd never seen her again.

It explained why Picasso had never travelled well. Ellie felt her heart go out to the pony. Every time he went into a horsebox, it must remind him in some way of that day when he had lost his mother. Was that why he wouldn't box now? But no, that didn't make sense. He had travelled many times since he was a foal. Something else must have happened more recently to make him so scared.

Do you know? she questioned Spirit.

A picture of a snake filled her mind.

A snake?

To be sure, she sent the picture back to Spirit.

His certainty was overwhelming. *Yes*.

Ellie saw a snake writhing in the straw on the floor of the horsebox behind Picasso's back legs.

No. She started to shake her head in confusion. *It can't be.*

Yes, she felt Spirit insist.

Ellie frowned. There couldn't have been a snake, there just couldn't. There weren't many snakes in this part of England and snakes hibernated in winter anyway. And even if by some remote chance there had been a snake in the horsebox, Picasso would certainly have killed it with his hooves and Joe or Stuart would have found it when they were clearing the straw out. She remembered the bay pony charging out of the box, neck lathered, rug askew, tail bandage left in a heap in the straw behind him . . .

Tail bandage.

Ellie's eyes widened suddenly. Was that it? Maybe the bandage had come loose while Picasso was travelling. She imagined it slowly unravelling as Len had driven along. The end would have brushed against his back legs. If Picasso had swished his tail, it could well have moved through the straw behind him like a snake. He'd been bitten when he was younger, Stuart had told her that, so if he'd thought there was a snake in the straw lining the box then it was no wonder he'd panicked and gone mad.

The importance of what she was figuring out gradually filtered through to Ellie. If it was true then maybe Picasso's fear of horseboxes could be cured. What they had to do was convince him there was no snake in the horsebox and help him find the confidence to go inside.

But then a new picture came to Ellie. She saw herself with Picasso, stroking him outside the horse-box, and then she saw Spirit inside it. Around him there seemed to be a warm and comforting glow. There was movement and a thud of hooves as Picasso walked up the ramp and joined him.

Ellie stared at Spirit. *You mean you think we could get him to go into the horsebox?*

Yes.

Ellie thought about the image Spirit had just sent. She'd tried talking to Picasso and it hadn't worked. Still, maybe she could try again. If she *could* communicate with him like she did with Spirit, then she could explain that there was no snake. And Spirit could help too. He seemed to be saying that if he was in the horsebox, maybe Picasso would go in once he realized there was no snake. She knew how much Picasso liked and trusted Spirit.

An idea suddenly shot through her like a firework going off. Maybe she *could* do another deal with her uncle – get him to agree to let her keep Spirit and not send him to the sale if she got Picasso into the horsebox.

It might just work. The plan filled Ellie's mind, blocking everything else out. But would her uncle agree?

There's only one way to find out, she realized.

Carried away by her excitement at the idea, she

kissed Spirit and hurried to the stable door. 'I'll be back soon. I've got to talk with Uncle Len!'

Ellie raced into the house, unable to think about anything but her plan. Her uncle was watching a football match on TV. He had a bottle of beer beside him and his feet were up on the footstool.

Ellie burst into the room, the idea spilling out of her even before she'd stopped. 'Uncle Len! If I get Picasso to go into the horsebox – if I cure him of being scared – will you let me keep Spirit?'

Len stared incredulously. 'Cure Picasso? What are you blithering on about?'

Ellie's heart pounded. 'If I get him to load, can I keep Spirit?'

Not even bothering to answer, her uncle turned the TV up with the remote.

'Please!' Ellie moved so she was standing in front of him and he couldn't see the screen. 'Let me try.'

'Get out the way.'

Ellie stood there stubbornly.

Len looked at her face. 'Oh, I see, you fancy your-self as some sort of flamin' horse whisperer now, do you?'

'No. I'm not a horse whisperer. But just give me one try. I think I might be able to do it.'

Please, please, please, she begged him inside her head.

Len hesitated, but then to her delight he nodded. 'Go on then. If it'll mean you'll leave me in peace, then yes, you can try tomorrow. But only tomorrow. I'm not wasting any more time after that. We'll sedate him and get him in that way.'

'But if I do it tomorrow, will you let me keep Spirit?' Ellie pushed. 'You won't send him to the sale on Thursday?'

'Yes . . . *if*.' The snort on the word made it clear Len felt she didn't have a chance. 'Now move yourself out of the ruddy way.'

'Thank you!' Ellie gasped, scooting hastily to one side just as Joe came into the room.

'What's going on?' he asked curiously.

Ellie dragged him through to the kitchen to explain. 'I've told your dad I'm going to get Picasso to go into the horsebox!' she said, her eyes shining. 'It'll be in exchange for keeping Spirit. Isn't that a brilliant idea?'

Through her excitement, she became aware that Joe was staring at her. 'You've said what?'

Ellie repeated it.

'But what was the point of saying that?' Joe looked as if she'd just told him she was going to walk on the moon. 'You'll never get Picasso in. Stuart and I have been trying all day. Dad's right, the only way now is to sedate him.'

Ellie wished she could explain it. 'I just think I

can.' *I hope I can*, she added to herself, the first few doubts beginning to push through her initial excitement.

'You're mental,' Joe said, shaking his head. An admiring smile pulled at his lips, though. 'But I wouldn't put anything past you. If anyone can do it, you can, Els. When are you going to try?'

Ellie took a breath. 'Tomorrow morning. First thing.' She went to the door.

'Where are you going now?' Joe asked in surprise.

'Back out to the stables.'

'It's gone nine o'clock!'

But Ellie was already out of the door. She needed to see Spirit. As she ran across the yard, reality began to sink in. It was a great idea, but would she be able to do it? She'd tried talking to Picasso before and it hadn't worked.

She slowed to a walk as she imagined her plan failing and her uncle laughing at her.

Don't think about that. The newspaper in the tack-room with the horse sale advert circled in red ink swam into her head. No, her plan *had* to work. She had to talk to Picasso and persuade him to go in.

Spirit was lying down in his stable now. Ellie sat down and put her arm over his neck, torn between her hopes and her doubts. 'I told Uncle Len I'd get Picasso in the box. I hope I did the right thing.'

As she settled down in the straw and leant against

his solid shoulder, she felt a bit calmer. At least she *had* a plan now – there was something she could try.

But would it work? Would she be able to talk to Picasso? Would she be able to get him into the lorry?

She heard Joe's voice in her head: *You'll never get Picasso in. Stuart and I have been trying all day.*

She hugged Spirit tightly. Tomorrow she would find out.

Chapter Thirteen

When Ellie finally got to bed that night, she slept fitfully, waking up every couple of hours. She heard the birds start to sing and saw the sky just starting to lighten. There would be at least an hour until everyone else was out on the yard. Maybe she should get up now and see if she could get Picasso into the horsebox before anyone else got up? The more she thought about trying to get him to load, the less she wanted an audience.

Trying not to make a sound, she crept down the stairs and out on to the yard. As she opened the door to the pony barn, there was a chorus of whinnies and the banging of hooves on doors. 'Later,' she told the other ponies as she hurried down the aisle. She fetched four long padded travelling boots and Picasso's headcollar.

The bay pony was very surprised to see her. He regarded her suspiciously.

'It's OK,' she murmured, putting everything down.

'There's nothing to worry about.' She let her mind clear and concentrated on sending out all the warmth she could. She imagined it wrapping round the bay pony, soothing and comforting him.

For a while nothing happened, but then she caught him starting to glance at her more and more often. Not warily now, but curiously.

She tried not to think of anything but him. *I'm here. I'm listening*, she told him in her head.

Gradually the feeling in the stable started to change. It was almost as if the air flowing around them was slowing down. She didn't get thoughts or feelings or pictures as she did with Spirit, but she got a sense of gradual connection – of some sort of link – between them.

Picasso seemed to feel something too. He came over and when she held out her hand he sniffed at it, breathing in and out.

'You'll be OK, Picasso,' she whispered. 'I promise. Just trust me. I know why you're scared of the horse-box and there's really no need to be. There's no snake.' Shutting her eyes, she sent him pictures of the horsebox, showing him there was no snake, showing him it had been his tail bandage touching his legs.

He snorted. She waited, hoping something more would happen. But nothing did. Standing up, she folded back his rug and ran her hands over him, stroking him all over. He accepted her touch, and as she returned to his head he lifted his muzzle to her face. She breathed gently into his nostrils and he breathed back.

Ellie ran a hand through his mane, thinking hard. She might not be talking to him in the way she did with Spirit, but she was sure there was some sort of connection between them. Maybe it would be enough? Maybe her thoughts had got through?

She hesitated. She would have liked to spend several days seeing if she could talk to him properly like she did with Spirit, but she didn't have the time. The deal was that she had to get him to load today. Should she risk it and try? It would be far better to do it while there was no one on the yard wanting to interfere. *Yes*, she decided. *I'll risk it.*

The yard was still deserted. She ran to the car park and let down both the side and rear ramps of the horsebox before going to fetch Spirit from his stable. He whinnied when he saw her coming.

'This is it, boy,' she whispered. 'I'm going to try and get Picasso in. I hope this is going to work.'

She led him down to the lorry, feeling a flicker of nervousness as she remembered how he had refused to load that day at the horse sale. But the relationship between them had grown immensely since then, and now he followed her up the ramp without hesitation.

Ellie's heart swelled as she realized how much he had changed in five weeks. Leaving Spirit pulling at one of the haynets that Stuart had put in there for the journey that morning, Ellie fetched Picasso. As they approached the horsebox, the bay pony tensed.

It's OK, she told him, letting him stop and placing a hand on his neck. *Nothing's going to hurt you. There's no snake, I promise. It was just your tail bandage before and now Spirit's in there.*

Spirit whinnied. Picasso hesitated and then stepped cautiously forward. Ellie walked beside him, not pulling or urging him, just murmuring soothingly. After a few steps he hesitated again. *Trust me*, she told him in her thoughts.

He walked forward. However, just as he got near to the ramp there was the sound of the back door opening and Joe, Luke and Len came out. She heard her uncle's voice saying something, then their laughs. They walked over and Picasso swung round.

Oh, no, Ellie thought, groaning inside. *Why did they have to come now?*

'Looks like we've come out just in time to see the horse whisperer in action,' commented Len loudly.

'Not that he's keeping his ears still enough for her to whisper into,' cracked Luke, glancing at Picasso's ears that were moving nervously back and forth now they were there.

'Let's watch and learn then, lads,' Len said, folding his arms across his chest.

For a moment, Ellie just wanted to run away. She couldn't bear them all watching to see if she failed. But then she lifted her chin. She wasn't going to fail. She also wasn't going to rush. She saw Joe's face, his eyes willing her on, and then she blocked out her audience. She talked to Picasso in her head.

It's all right, she told him. *We can take as long as you want.*

Gradually she felt him tune into her.

I won't let anything hurt you. Spirit's waiting for you. There's nothing bad in the horsebox, I promise. You'll be safe with me and Spirit.

She hoped her words were getting through, wished he would reply as Spirit did. All she had to go by was the fact she could sense his tension was easing. His head lowered and he nudged her with his nose.

'I'll get behind him,' offered Luke.

Ellie opened her mouth in alarm to stop him, but, before she could, Joe had grabbed Luke's arm.

'No! Ellie's doing this on her own.'

Luke glanced down at Joe's hand on his arm and then at his face. His eyes narrowed, but he stepped back. 'What's it to do with you?'

'Just let her do it,' insisted Joe. 'Give her a chance. I bet she can.'

Ellie felt a rush of gratitude for his confidence.

162

Picasso's eyes met hers and then he stepped towards the box. She kept him on a loose rein, just repeating over and over again in her head: *It's OK. Spirit's there. He's waiting. There's no snake.*

As they reached the ramp, Spirit called again. With an answering whicker, Picasso stepped on to the ramp and stopped. Ellie felt as if the world paused for a second and then suddenly, without a fuss, the pony pricked his ears and walked quickly inside.

Ellie stopped in front of him. Her heart was in her mouth. She could hardly believe she'd done it – she'd got him in! She heard Joe's delighted exclamation, her uncle's snort of astonishment, and then she came to life and started patting Picasso over and over again as he touched noses with Spirit. 'Oh, good boy! I told you there was nothing to be frightened of. And thank you.' She turned to Spirit and kissed his nose. He looked up at her through his long forelock and she kissed him again before swinging round in delight. Luke and her uncle were stunned. Ellie could have giggled as she saw their faces. Joe was grinning, jogging over.

'That was brilliant! Well done, Els! I knew you could do it.'

'No use just getting him in once, though,' Luke called.

'I can do it again,' she said, needled. Touching Picasso's neck, she led him back down the ramp and walked him in a circle. Then she clicked her tongue and led him back inside. This time she had absolute confidence he would follow her and he did. He stopped and she tied him up and put the partition across. Then she turned and looked challengingly at her uncle.

He still had his arms folded, but now he was nodding slowly. 'You did it, lass. Full credit to you.'

She knew from his face that he had never expected her to succeed and she felt a sweet rush of triumph.

'It was a good idea to put that grey of yours inside,' he went on. He looked at Spirit with narrowed eyes. 'Stuart's been saying the other horses like him.'

'Can I keep him?' Her heart was in her throat. She didn't care that her uncle thought the only reason Picasso had loaded was because of Spirit; she just wanted the answer. Her heart thudded in her ears as she waited for her uncle to reply. Each second felt like an hour, and then Len nodded.

'A deal's a deal. He can stay. He might even prove himself useful.'

Ellie gasped. As her uncle and Luke walked away, Joe jumped on to the ramp.

'That's brilliant! Oh, Ellie. You did it!'

'I can't believe it! I can't believe it!' Ellie's voice rose and she hugged Spirit. 'You can stay!' she told him joyously.

'Dad's coming back,' warned Joe.

Ellie swung round. Fear suddenly gripped her. Her uncle hadn't changed his mind, had he?

He pointed his finger at her. 'You'd better go and get your show clothes. And, Joe, tell Stuart to get that pony plaited up. You've both got a show to go to.'

Chapter Fourteen

The next few hours passed in a blur for Ellie. Almost before she knew it, she found herself in the cab of the horsebox, travelling to the show with Joe and Stuart, while Len and Luke followed in one car and Eliza and Carey, Len's clients, followed in another. Barney, Picasso, Darcey and Alfie were groomed to perfection, their gleaming coats and neat plaits protected by smart maroon rugs and hoods. They were wearing special leather show headcollars with maroon leadropes, and all the horses apart from Picasso had matching maroon tail bandages. Ellie had explained that it would be better not to put a tail bandage on him from now on. Even Spirit, who was with them to keep Picasso calm, was rugged up. 'I'm not having a horse coming out of my lorry that doesn't look smart,' Len had said as he'd sent Ellie off to groom him quickly before they left.

She could hardly believe she was about to take part in her first show in England. Part of her wished she could just be spending the day with Spirit, maybe taking him for another bareback ride, just being with him, enjoying the moment. But another part of her was full of excitement. Picasso looked amazing and she couldn't wait to take him in the ring. And at least Spirit was there with her.

The show was at a huge equestrian centre, with some of the classes held indoors and some out. While Stuart and Luke unloaded the ponies and got them tacked up, and Len went to register and pick up the numbers, Joe quickly showed Ellie around.

There was an outdoor ring and two indoor rings, as well as a working-in area. Everywhere Ellie looked there were beautiful horses and ponies, their coats velvet-soft and shining, their tack gleaming in the March sun. People wandered around, chatting and talking on their phones. Small girls on beautiful lead-rein ponies were having red hair ribbons tied and their boots polished. In the working-in area, trainers were putting the practice fences up and down, and carrying round wicker baskets full of grooming tools.

'That's the working hunter ring,' said Joe, pointing out a ring where a pony was jumping round a course of jumps for one judge, and then a further smaller ring where there was another pony performing an individual show for another judge. Joe checked the rider's number. 'We should go and work Picasso and

Barney in and then come back and walk the course. Your class will be before mine.'

They headed back to the horsebox and tacked the ponies up. Keeping their jeans and jackets on over their show clothes, Ellie and Joe worked them in with Len watching. Picasso was full of energy and jumpy, but gradually he calmed down.

When it came to walking the course, Joe was a great help, pointing out where Ellie would need to take care, where she should push on and how many strides she should aim for between the jumps. Lots of the other riders seemed to know him and called out greetings.

'You just want to mind the upright at the end,' he told Ellie. 'Picasso can get a bit full of himself when he thinks the course is over, and it's the type of fence that will come down easily.' Ellie took it all in. She felt as if she was bubbling inside; she couldn't wait to get started!

When she went back to the box, Luke was expertly putting the finishing touches to Picasso, adding a final layer of special black dye to his hooves and rubbing over his coat with a soft cloth. 'He's just about ready.'

'Thanks,' she said, glad that he had dropped his usual goading manner for the show.

Spirit was tied up next to Picasso, looking around curiously. Ellie gave him a hug.

'You'd better get ready too,' Luke told her. 'If you're late for the ring, Len will kill you.'

Ellie slipped into the grooms' quarters of the box and pulled off her old jeans. She had her show jodh-purs underneath. She replaited her hair in a single neat plait, put on her red tie, her brown jodhpur boots, her tweed jacket and leather gloves. Putting on her velvet hat, she looked at herself in the mirror. Her eyes were glowing.

Opening the door, she jumped down from the horsebox. Luke grinned. 'You're enjoying this, aren't you?'

She nodded, for once almost lost for words with the excitement and nerves.

'I love it too,' he admitted. 'It's good having some-one else here who enjoys it. I know Joe would sooner stay at home. I wish I was riding today.' He undid Picasso's headcollar. 'Here. On you get.'

She mounted and went to check the girth, but Luke caught her arm. 'No, wait. You'll get grease on your gloves. Let me.' He checked, running his finger between the girth and Picasso's side. It wasn't quite tight enough and he moved her leg forward, lifting up the saddle flap. As she looked down on his dark head while he hiked the girth up another hole, his shoulder holding her leg out of the way, she wished he could always be this nice.

'Thanks,' she said.

'My pleasure.' For just a moment there was the hint of his usual mocking expression, but then his face relaxed and he let her leg fall back into place. He swept the cloth over her boots where they had brushed against Picasso's neck, removing the last specks of dust. 'Just go out there and win.'

'I'll try.' She clicked her tongue and Picasso moved off.

Spirit whinnied.

Ellie smiled. She knew it was silly, but she was sure he was wishing her good luck too.

As soon as Ellie rode into the ring, her nerves vanished. She cantered round, feeling Picasso's eagerness. 'Steady, steady,' she breathed as they approached the first jump. He flew over, his ears pricked. Jump followed jump. She remembered Joe's advice at the final fence and was ready when she felt him speed up. Now was not the time for one of his infamous bucks. Keeping him firmly in hand, she placed him perfectly at the fence. He cleared it by miles and she rode on strongly, keeping a good hold on his head. She ended the round with her heart singing. A clear round! Her uncle met her at the exit with a rare smile.

'Good work, lass,' he said, clapping Picasso's neck.

There was a grey pony in the smaller ring, doing its individual show for the second judge. In the individual show they had to walk, trot, canter and gallop. Ellie waited for her turn and, as the grey left, she rode in. Picasso performed beautifully, floating across the ground, his neck arched, reaching perfectly for the bit before doing a really fast gallop. Joe had told Ellie that Picasso loved being in the ring, and she could feel it exuding from the pony's every pore. He made it easy for her to ride as well as she possibly could, speeding up and slowing down whenever she asked.

She finished by bowing to the judge, and then Joe and her uncle helped her whisk Picasso's saddle off so she could lead him back into the ring for the judge to check him over one last time. Picasso stood like a statue and didn't put a foot wrong as she then walked and trotted him in-hand. At the end of the class, all the ponies were called back into the ring together by the steward. They lined up and Picasso was pronounced the winner.

Ellie could hardly contain her delight as the judge hooked a red rosette on to the string that held her number in place and congratulated her. Her first show and she had won – or at least Picasso had! She led the lap of honour while everyone clapped loudly.

Getting out of the ring, she leapt off and hugged Picasso. The next second Joe, Luke and Len were congratulating her.

'He was awesome!' she gasped.

'So were you!' said Joe.

Luke grinned. 'I knew you'd enjoy it.'

'It was a good ride,' said Len, nodding approvingly. 'A very good ride.'

Ellie took Picasso back to the horsebox, glowing with pride, but her showing day wasn't over. Later on she had to take him in the working hunter pony championship for the ponies who had been placed first and second in their classes. They came second overall in that and were presented with another even larger rosette for being Reserve Champion, even beating Joe and Barney who had won their class too.

Afterwards, Ellie and Joe rode the ponies back to the car park. They took it in turns to get changed in the living quarters and then rubbed Barney and Picasso down before giving them some water, rugging them up and settling them with fresh haynets in the lorry.

'What a day!' said Ellie dazedly as they went back into the living area and tidied up.

Joe grinned at her as he stowed their hats in one of the lockers. 'And to think just a few months ago you wouldn't even ride the ponies.'

'Yeah.' Ellie shook her head. So much had happened in the last few months. Spirit. The ponies. Everything. She remembered how she had felt when she first arrived at High Peak Stables, how desolate she had been.

Overwhelmed by the memory, Ellie rubbed her arm across her eyes.

'Are you OK?' Joe said, coming over and putting a hand on her shoulder.

She nodded, swallowing hard.

'Really?'

As she glanced into his greeny-grey eyes, Ellie felt her stomach curl. They stared at each other for a moment and then Joe gently brushed a loose strand of hair back from Ellie's face. Almost without realizing what she was doing, she stepped forward. He lowered his head instinctively and she rose on tiptoe to meet him.

Just then, the handle on the jockey door turned with a rattle. They leapt apart as if someone had just thrown scalding water over them.

The door opened. Luke was standing there. 'Alfie's about to go in the Intermediate Championship,' he announced. 'Are you two going to come and watch?' He seemed to pick up on the tension. He looked from one to the other. 'What's going on?'

'Going on? Nothing,' Joe said, grabbing a whip off the floor and throwing it into a bucket with the other whips. 'We . . . we were just putting stuff away.'

Ellie's heart was pounding. 'Yes. Just tidying up a bit.' She turned so Luke couldn't see her burning cheeks.

'Well, come and see the championship then,' said Luke, giving Ellie one last penetrating stare.

'Sure.' Joe went to the door. 'Coming, Ellie?'

Ellie waited as Luke had turned and begun walking back towards the show.

'Joe . . .' she breathed, wondering what had just happened. Reaching out, she touched his hand. Their eyes met.

'Come on,' Joe said softly, after a moment. 'We'd really better go, Ellie.'

She nodded, her heart still beating wildly against her ribs.

He jumped down from the horsebox. She scrambled down the steps after him, and studiously avoiding each other's gaze, they followed Luke back across the car park.

Sunset . . .

Ellie walked beside Spirit along the lane as the sun slowly sank down in the sky. She rested her hand on his shoulders, feeling his muscles move beneath her palm. As always, when she was with him, and just him, she felt a sense of peace – of coming home.

Her thoughts mulled over the day. The show had been so much fun, but then there had been the moment in the horsebox with Joe . . .

It was only because I was upset, she told herself. *It was hard thinking about everything that's happened – Mum, Dad, almost losing Spirit.*

Her fingers played in Spirit's long mane. She must stop thinking about it. Joe was her friend, that was all. Pushing the memory deep down, she remembered the rest of the show. It had been fantastic to win the class and quite weird to get on with Luke for a change. Ellie shook her head. She'd never met anyone who she could like so much one minute and then hate the next. But he'd been like a different person while they had been at the show. Excitement bubbled through her as she suddenly remembered the moment when she had won the class. She couldn't wait until the next time.

Sensitive to her moods as always, Spirit pushed against her.

She patted him. 'Joe was right in the horsebox, Spirit,' she told him. 'So much has changed in just a few months. Not just the riding and the shows, of course, but having you and being able to talk to you, and now being able to keep you and also being able to communicate with Picasso too. Everything's different.'

Spirit lifted his nose and explored her face with his muzzle. Ellie felt a rush of overpowering love and sighed. Without doubt, the thing that mattered most was keeping him. Everything else could change, but as long as she had Spirit she knew her life would be complete.

She remembered the bleak landscape she had arrived to, less than three months ago. The ground had been hard with frost, the wind bitter, the trees' branches bare. But now the sun was shining, the fields were full of lambs, some bouncing, others feeding, tails waggling, while their mothers grazed. Bright yellow daffodils waved along the grass verge and the leaves on the trees were new and green.

The months ahead felt as if they were stretching

out in front of her like the golden rays of the sun stretching across the fields. What would they hold? There would be more shows. Maybe she would be able to learn how to talk properly to other horses. That was such an amazing idea. Then there would be Spirit, of course. She would do more with him, ride him with a saddle and bridle, learn more from him, love him and be loved by him.

A picture of the first time she had seen him flashed into her mind, and she remembered the feeling she'd had that day, as if she'd always known him.

You're mine, she had promised him. *Forever.*

She had meant it then. She knew it now. Their eyes met and she lost herself again in his gaze, feeling a wonderful sense of security. Whatever the future held, she would meet it with him.

The winter had passed; spring was here.

Special Thanks . . .

There are so many people to thank for Ellie and Spirit's story. My agent, the wonderful Philippa Milnes-Smith, who encouraged me to write it from the very first moment we met, and her fabulous assistant, Holly Vitow. My editor, Lindsey Heaven, for her passion, skill and general loveliness even when we have been arguing – I know it's only because you care! To everyone at Puffin who has put time into turning my story into proper books, especially Wendy Tse for her edits and patience and Katy Finch for the perfect covers.

On the horse front, I owe a massive thank you to Julie Templeton and Fiona Wallace of the Julie Templeton show team. They showed me around their amazing yard and patiently answered so many questions about showing, willingly giving up their busy time – any stretching of showing reality is down to me! The many non-fiction books by Mark Rashid, an incredible horseman, have also been invaluable, as have the books by horse healers Julie Dicker and Magrit Coates.

And then there are the thanks to everyone else in my life who has been involved with this story. To Peter, Iola, Amany and Spike for putting up with me writing all the time, particularly to Peter for the endless love, support and inspiration – you are my guiding light and I love you for it! To the writing friends who make my day-to-day writing life so much more fun than it would be otherwise: Lee Weatherly, Julie Sykes, Liz Kessler, Dave Gatward and Ann Bryant (particular thanks to Lee, Liz, Ann and Julie for reading various drafts, seeing what I wanted to write and helping me iron out problems). To all the rest of the Scattered Authors, the most wonderful and generous group of writers. To my non-writing friends who keep me sane: Suzanne, Emma, Sarah, Jo, Debs, Sandra, Caroline, Wendy and Elaine. And to DB, wherever you are, for the light and the shadows you brought – this story would not be here without you. Thank you. Most of all, though, I have an immense debt of gratitude to the horses and dogs who are no longer with me, especially Tan, Bramble and Poppy. All animals are special, but some touch your life and heart in a whole different way. Those three taught me so much and I miss them all every day. Finally a huge thank you to everyone who reads Ellie and Spirit's story and enjoys it – listen and maybe you will hear an answer one day . . .

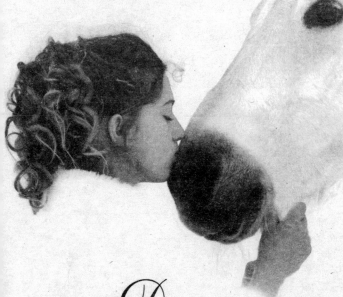

Now Ellie's found him,
she'll never let go . . .

*D*iscover each of the
books in this stunning

Loving
Spirit
quartet.